THE ICE

When Leane Forrest lost confidence in her nursing ability, she needed an easy job to help her regain it. Looking after the actress Romaine Hart, in Switzerland, would have been ideal—except for that bad-mannered Doctor Adam Blake, who always stayed so close to Romaine's side, and treated Leane with contempt. How could she endure three months in his company?

*Books you will enjoy
in our Doctor – Nurse series*

PICTURE OF A DOCTOR by Lisa Cooper
NURSE MARIA by Marion Collin
NURSE AT WHISPERING PINES by Elizabeth Petty
WISH WITH THE CANDLES by Betty Neels
STAFF NURSE AT ST MILDRED'S by Janet Ferguson
THE RUSTLE OF BAMBOO by Celine Conway
OMEN FOR LOVE by Esther Boyd
JET NURSE by Muriel Janes
PRIZE OF GOLD by Hazel Fisher
DOCTOR ON BOARD by Betty Beaty
FIRST YEAR LOVE by Clare Lavenham
SURGEON IN CHARGE by Betty Neels
SURGEON'S CHALLENGE by Helen Upshall
ATTACHED TO DOCTOR MARCHMONT by Juliet Shore
DOCTORS IN CONFLICT by Sonia Deane
NURSE AT BARBAZON by Kathryn Blair
ANGELS IN RED by Lisa Cooper
EVEN DOCTORS WEEP by Anne Vinton
THE GEMEL RING by Betty Neels

THE ICEBERG ROSE

BY

SARAH FRANKLIN

MILLS & BOON LIMITED
London . Sydney . Toronto

*First published in Great Britain 1981
by Mills & Boon Limited, 15-16 Brook's Mews,
London W1A 1DR*

© Sarah Franklin 1981

Australian copyright 1981
Philippine copyright 1981

ISBN 0 263 73458 7

All the characters in this book have no existence outside the imagination of the Author, and have no relation whatsoever to anyone bearing the same name or names. They are not even distantly inspired by any individual known or unknown to the Author, and all the incidents are pure invention.

The text of this publication or any part thereof may not be reproduced or transmitted in any form or by any means, electronic or mechanical, including photocopying, recording, storage in an information retrieval system, or otherwise, without the written permission of the publisher.

This book is sold subject to the condition that it shall not, by way of trade or otherwise, be lent, resold, hired out or otherwise circulated without the prior consent of the publisher in any form of binding or cover other than that in which it is published and without a similar condition including this condition being imposed on the subsequent purchaser.

Set in 10 on 11½ pt Monophoto Plantin

*Made and printed in Great Britain by
Richard Clay (The Chaucer Press), Ltd.,
Bungay, Suffolk*

CHAPTER ONE

LEANE glanced at her watch for what seemed the hundredth time and shifted her position in the chair. The last candidate had gone in for her interview, leaving her alone. It was her turn next and she felt the familiar butterflies begin to stir in the pit of her stomach.

She opened the folded magazine that lay on her lap and looked again at the advertisement ringed in red pencil: '*Young woman with nursing experience required as nurse/companion to lady travelling abroad.*' She had replied to it on impulse three weeks ago and then promptly forgotten about it. Indeed she had been surprised when she had received the telephone message last night, asking her to present herself for interview at the Winchester Hotel at two o'clock this afternoon. If she had thought about it at all during the past days it had only been to conclude that by this time the job must have been filled.

'Aren't you pleased?' Bridget, her flat-mate, had asked exasperatedly. 'After all, Lee, it's a whole month since you left St Ann's. Do try to show some enthusiasm.'

And she had tried, but it hadn't been easy—nothing was nowadays. Ever since that dreadful night in Casualty, it had seemed as though her life were falling apart at the seams. She looked again at her watch—four-thirty. She had been here two and a half hours. She hoped it would be worth it. There had been a lot of people after the job, but then the salary offered was extremely generous, so it wasn't surprising.

The door opposite opened and a thin-faced woman of about thirty came out and glanced at Leane.

'I think it's your turn now.' She sniffed and departed through the door that led to the lift.

Leane stood up and moved hesitantly to the door left open by the woman. She had just reached it when a cross-looking man appeared, almost colliding with her. He was tall and broad-shouldered, with dark hair, and his thick eyebrows came together in a frown as the sheaf of papers he was carrying fluttered to the floor.

'For Heaven's sake!' he exploded. 'If you're coming in please come—don't dither about!'

'I'm sorry.' Leane bent to gather up the papers. She handed them to him, meeting the dark eyes directly. 'I wasn't aware that there was any great hurry. I've already been here for two and a half hours. Would you like me to come back tomorrow?'

'Oh, God forbid!' he said, raising his eyes to the ceiling. 'I've been interviewing since ten o'clock this morning. Don't wish any more on me!'

He held the door as she passed through into another, smaller room furnished with a desk and two chairs.

'I expect you must have made your choice by now,' Leane said hesitantly, her hand on the back of the chair opposite his. 'Perhaps I'm just wasting your time. Please don't think you have to interview me just because of what I said.'

He looked up at her from behind the desk. He now wore a pair of dark-rimmed spectacles through which he had been scanning her application. A flicker of irritation crossed his brow as he pulled them off.

'Oh, do sit down and let's get on with it, Miss—Miss——' his eyes searched a list before him on the desk.

'Forrest—Leane Forrest,' she supplied stiffly. She was wondering who this man was and why he was interviewing the candidates for the job. As though he read her thoughts, he said:

'I'm Dr Adam Blake, and for the moment I'm acting as medical advisor to the lady offering the post you have applied for.' He looked up at her. 'Please sit down, Miss Forrest, and stop hovering. I'm sure this won't take long.'

Leane did as she was told with some misgivings. It seemed to her that the interview was a mere formality and Dr Blake's attitude suggested that the whole thing was a bore to him.

'I see from your application that you're an S.R.N. and that until recently you were nursing at St Ann's.' He raised a quizzical eyebrow at her.

'That is correct.'

He pulled off the spectacles again and leaned back in his chair. 'Then what on earth makes you apply for a post of this kind?'

She met his critical eyes unflinchingly. 'I feel like a change,' she said.

'You mean you intend to go in for private nursing?'

She shrugged. 'At present I wouldn't mind what job I took, but as nursing is what I know——'

He frowned. 'If you don't mind my saying so, Nurse Forrest, you don't sound very dedicated.'

Leane coloured hotly. 'I don't know how I sound, Dr Blake, but I do know that I'm good at my job. You'll find a reference from my Senior Nursing Officer enclosed with my application.'

'I know—I've read it,' he said coolly. 'I suppose you realise that this job is temporary? That is the reason for the generous salary mentioned in the advertisement. It was an unfortunate move, putting that figure into print. It has attracted a great many unsuitable people.'

Leane bit back a hasty retort, but said stiffly: 'So I would imagine. It wasn't the salary that attracted me.'

'Indeed I hope not.' He looked at her. 'Well, I'd better tell you a little about it. The lady in question will be travelling to Switzerland in three weeks' time to undergo an operation. She intends to stay for a period of three months and will require a nurse—companion; someone who's prepared to be kind in a human, as well as a professional way. I'll be frank with you, Nurse. I wasn't expecting any applications from S.R.Ns. In my opinion a trained nurse like yourself—recently qualified—owes a not inconsiderable debt to the hospital that trained her.'

Leane rose shakily to her feet. 'As you are not to be my employer, Doctor, I don't see that it is any of your business what job I take as long as I'm prepared to carry it out to the best of my ability. But as I'm obviously not what you're looking for, I'll leave.' She walked to the door.

'Come back here at once, Nurse Forrest!' He barked out the command and Leane stopped in her tracks and turned. The years of discipline made her react automatically and immediately she checked, furious with herself for her instinctive obedience. But it was too late.

'Sit down again,' he instructed. 'I haven't said that you are unsuitable and I would like to continue—if you have no objection.' His tone was faintly sarcastic and she would have given anything to have been in the lift at that moment, speeding streetwards. With a slight nod she sat in the chair opposite and waited.

'Would you care to give me your reasons for leaving St Ann's?' he asked, his tone a little softer.

She sighed unhappily. 'I—I had an unpleasant experience,' she said inadequately.

'What kind of unpleasant experience?' he probed.

She bit her lip. 'A patient—died.'

His eyebrows shot up. 'That, I'm afraid is an occupational hazard. We all have to lose patients sometimes—and it's always unpleasant.'

She shook her head impatiently. 'I know. Of course I was prepared for that, but this was—different.' She looked down at the clenched hands twisting in her lap. There was a short silence between them, then he said:

'And for that reason alone you opted out of nursing?'

Leane frowned. He made it all sound so feeble and of course there was more to it—much more, impossible to explain to this unfeeling man opposite her, even if she had wanted to.

'The situation—the facts of the case,' she faltered.

He held up his hand. 'Spare me those. I'll take your word for it. Right, so you're looking for a—shall we say a little respite, while you consider your future. Is that it, Nurse?'

She nodded. 'You could say that.'

He turned over her application, then looked up at her. 'No romantic entanglements? No impatient fiancé waiting for your return?'

'No!'

The expressive eyebrows rose again. 'You sound ominously emphatic. A broken romance, maybe?'

She stared at him. 'Is this relevant, Doctor?'

He had the grace to colour slightly. 'No, not entirely. I apologise, Nurse.'

'And I'd prefer to be called Miss at present,' she added, rising. 'Will that be all, Dr Blake?'

He stood to face her across the desk. 'I think so.' He picked up a piece of paper from the desk. 'It may interest you to know that the lady I represent has put on the top of her list of requirements: "Must be lively and attractive."' He glanced at her. 'I think we can safely say that you meet those requirements, Miss Forrest. I'll be in touch. Good afternoon.'

She nodded. 'Good afternoon, Doctor.' Was it his way of making up for his rudeness? Or was there a veiled insult behind the remark? She decided she didn't much care either way. All she wanted was to get back to the flat and make herself a cup of tea.

The rush hour was well and truly under way by the time she got to the underground and as she stood wedged between the commuters she thought back over the interview. It really couldn't have been more disastrous. The man had brought out the worst in her, making her look awkward and gauche. She had objected to his obvious references to the size of the salary, too, though she could understand his anxiety on that count. But his probing into her reasons for leaving St Ann's had opened old wounds, and she found with dismay that they were as painful as ever.

Hanging from her strap on the swaying train, Leane was suddenly back in the Casualty department on that terrible Saturday night. Her palms became sticky at the thought of it. St Ann's was in the East End, and Casualty was a notorious place on a Saturday night. Leane had been a Staff Nurse for only two months when she found herself on duty there on that Saturday evening last February.

It had been a fairly quiet night to begin with, then there had been an emergency, an accident involving two cars and a bus. Sister had put her in charge while she helped the doctor in Minor Ops and dealt with admissions. Everyone was busy; then to cap everything, two youths had brought in a third suffering from a bad stab wound, inflicted in a street brawl, and Leane had to deal not only with the patient and his loudly arguing friends, but also with an eager young policeman who was trying to obtain a statement from them. During all this a nurse had pointed the man out to her and she had glimpsed him briefly.

He had looked just like any other drunk as he

leaned there against the wall and she had told the nurse to put him into a cubicle. 'With luck he'll have slept it off before I get round to him,' she'd thought to herself.

But when she finally did look into the cubicle it was to find the man collapsed on the floor, his eyes glazed and his breath rasping in his throat. She had called for help but by the time they had lifted him on to the examination couch he had stopped breathing. Resuscitation was useless.

It was all over so quickly that it left her feeling numb and shocked. Although a post mortem had revealed the cause of death as 'cardiac arrest due to a coronary obstruction' which could have occurred at any time, Leane felt the responsibility keenly. She was told that she had done everything possible and was not in any way to blame, but she could not lose the feeling of guilt. She should have examined the man as soon as she saw that he was unsteady on his feet, and not taken it for granted that he was drunk. The fact that she had been rushed off her feet was no excuse.

After that night nothing had been the same, her confidence was shattered. She had made stupid mistakes, dropped things; her memory had begun playing her tricks and at last, after a month of uncertainty and heart-searching, she had handed in her notice.

Leane came to with a jerk as the train drew into Liverpool Street station and the occupants of the carriage began to squeeze out on to the platform like toothpaste out of a tube. As she gave up her ticket and came up into the spring sunshine again she was still thinking about St Ann's and the life she had severed herself from.

She hadn't realised that she would feel so bereft and out of things once her notice was up and she had joined the ranks of the unemployed. And then, of course, there was Tony.

She had been going out with Tony Gifford ever since she was a probationer and he was in his third year at medical school. Now he was a houseman on the team of Mr Forbes-Leighton, the E.N.T. consultant. He had shown disappointment when she had 'thrown in the sponge', as he put it, and since then things between them had been decidedly cool. Yes, all in all it would be better—much better, Leane told herself—if she got right away from all the old associations and made a completely new start, though it was easier said than done!

'Well—how did it go?' Bridget confronted her, bright-eyed and rosy after her day-time sleep. In her blue dressing-gown she looked about twelve, and as Leane stood regaining her breath after climbing the three flights of stairs to the flat, she marvelled at how fresh her friend looked after her short rest. When she was on nights she always felt dead at this time of the day.

'Oh come on, I'm dying to know!' Bridget pulled her into the sitting-room. 'Did you get the job? What was the old dear like?'

Leane laughed in spite of herself. 'You might give me time to get my breath back! And the "old dear", as you call her, wasn't there. Her doctor was doing the interviewing—and he didn't approve of yours truly one little bit!' She pulled off her coat and went into the hall to hang it up. 'Is there a cuppa, Bridget? I'm absolutely parched. I hit the rush hour and——'

She broke off as Bridget pushed her firmly into a chair.

'You'll get your tea in good time. First I want to hear all about the job and the interview, so you may as well get it over with!'

Leane sighed. 'Nothing to tell, really.'

Bridget stood looking down at her, hands on hips. 'You mean someone else got it?'

'No—I don't know. He said he'd be in touch—but I haven't got it, I'm sure of that.'

'What was he like?'

'In a word—rude!'

Bridget pulled a face. 'Why should he be rude?'

Leane went on to recount the interview blow by blow, and when she had finished Bridget slumped in a chair. 'Phew! I reckon you deserve a double whisky after that lot, but a strong cup of tea will have to do.' She disappeared into the adjoining kitchen and continued the conversation above the whistle of the kettle.

'A good job it's not him you'll be working for! How old is the woman—and what's wrong with her?'

'He didn't say,' Leane called back. 'I don't suppose it matters anyway. I told you, I won't have got the job. He made no bones about telling me that he totally disapproved of me.'

Bridget reappeared with the tray, her eyes twinkling. 'What about that bit about you being "lively and attractive", though? That sounded promising.'

'You wouldn't think so if you'd been there,' Leane told her as she sipped her tea gratefully. 'He made it sound as though they were the only assets I had. He said I was undedicated and that I

14

owed a——' She frowned, trying to remember his exact words. 'A not inconsiderable debt to the hospital that trained me! He made me sound like a lazy little gold-digger.'

Bridget pulled a face into her teacup. 'He sounds like a pompous old twit to me!'

Leane laughed, feeling suddenly light-hearted again. 'That's a pretty good description—except that he's not old.'

'Oh?' Bridget looked interested. 'How old?'

'About thirtyish.'

'Mmm—good-looking?'

Leane considered, her head on one side. 'Yes, I suppose so, but he spoils it by frowning all the time. Besides, he has a cleft in his chin and I always think that's a sign of conceit.'

'Dark or fair?' Bridget asked.

'Dark.'

'And I'll bet he has brooding brown eyes.' Bridget drew her knees up to her chin and hugged them. 'Wow! He sounds the mean, moody and magnificent type. I wish I'd gone with you now.'

Leane drained her cup. 'Well, I don't suppose either of us will ever get the chance to find out what type he is.' She got up and picked up the tea-tray. 'And for my part I couldn't care less. So let's get the supper, Bridget Sullivan, or you'll have Sister after you again for being late!'

After Bridget had gone off to report for night duty the flat was quiet and Leane reflected that she would miss her friend very much when the time came for her to move on. They had done their training together and taken their S.R.N. exams in the same week. But Bridget had failed hers and would have to try again.

The bright, pretty Irish girl had a good effect on Leane who was of a more serious nature. When things went wrong she always managed to put the world back into perspective; she took life's ups and downs as they came, never allowing herself to take anything too seriously. The patients adored her, Sisters shook their heads despairingly over her and she made the doctors laugh. If only I had been more like her, Leane mused, maybe I'd still be happily nursing at St Ann's now instead of groping in the dark for a new future.

She did a few chores, watched television for a while and was just thinking of having an early night when the door bell rang. She got up to answer it with a sigh, expecting to see Mrs Jones from upstairs again, asking to borrow the iron. When she found Tony waiting outside she was surprised. He hadn't telephoned or contacted her at all for a fortnight. He smiled a little sheepishly.

'Hello, Lee. Can I come in?'

She stood back, holding the door open. 'Of course. It's nice to see you, Tony.'

He followed her into the sitting-room and she noticed his wet raincoat for the first time. 'Would you like to take your mac off? I didn't know it had started to rain.'

He nodded, shrugging out of the mac and giving it to her. Their eyes met for a moment, and at once Leane knew that something was wrong. They had known each other for a long time and she didn't remember seeing him so ill at ease.

'Would you like a cup of coffee?' she asked. 'I

was just going to make some.'

He smiled. 'That would be nice.'

In the kitchen she called out to him as she made the coffee: 'How are things with you? It seems an age since I saw you.'

But he answered monosyllabically. It wasn't until they were seated, the tray between them on the table, that he began to get round to the point.

'Lee—I don't know if you've heard any—hospital gossip about me lately?'

She looked up at him. 'No. But then I'm not around the hospital much any more, am I?'

'Bridget is.'

'Bridget doesn't gossip,' she told him.

He paused for a moment, turning the coffee mug between his hands as though warming them. 'I know—but if the gossip were based on fact she might pass it on.'

'What is it you're trying to tell me, Tony?' she asked directly. 'I wish you'd come to the point. It surely can't be as bad as all that.'

But suddenly there was no need for him to tell her, she knew what he had come to say to her as clearly as though it were written on his forehead. She waited, looking at him intently and when he didn't go on she prompted: 'You want us to stop seeing each other—that's it, isn't it?'

He winced at her directness, then nodded reluctantly. 'I feel awful, Lee. I should have come clean with you a long time ago. You see, there's——'

'Someone else?' she supplied. 'I think I've known for some time anyway, Tony. We haven't been—well, close, for months now, have we? I suppose we just—grew out of each other. Is it anyone I know?'

He cleared his throat, looking at the floor. 'Not exactly. Her name is Elizabeth Forbes-Leighton. I met her at a party just after you left St Ann's.'

The name was too distinctive for her not to recognise it. 'Any relation to E.N.T. Forbes-Leighton?' she asked lightly.

He coloured slightly. 'Daughter, as a matter of fact, but that has nothing to do with——' He trailed off. 'That was what I meant about gossip, Lee, but it's unfounded, really. We're in love. It wouldn't matter to me whose daughter she was.'

She smiled calmly. 'I'm glad for you both. And thank you for telling me, Tony.'

He looked at her, his brows drawn together in a frown of concern, but she read the unmistakable relief in his eyes.

'You—really don't mind?'

She began to put the mugs on to the tray to give her hands something to do. 'I've no right to mind, have I? There was never anything binding between us.'

He sighed. 'But we have known each other a long time.' He looked at her. 'We had some good times together, Lee. It sounds funny, but I shall miss you.'

It was the most final thing he had said and the most dismissive. Leane's heart gave a lurch. She stood up and gave him her hand.

'I hope you'll both be very happy, Tony.'

He took her hand and held on to it for a long moment. 'What will you do? Will you be all right?'

Her eyebrows rose. 'Of course! Did you think I

was going to throw myself out of a window? It's as I said, Tony. We grew out of each other, just as I've grown out of hospital life. I've already got another job. Actually, I'm going abroad to do some private nursing. I shall be gone within the month.'

Inwardly she gasped at her rashness. Why on earth had she told such a crashing lie? Pride, she supposed.

Tony looked chastened. 'Well—I'll wish you all the best. Goodbye, Lee.'

After he'd gone she stood for a long time at the window. She'd seen him come out of the building and run down the steps, putting up the collar of his mac against the rain as he went. Then he disappeared into the throng of traffic swishing past on the wet road.

A few moments later he reappeared on the other side of the road getting into a little red sports car. A laughing blonde girl sat at the wheel. They drove away looking happy and Leane turned from the window into the room again. What did she feel? she asked herself. Hurt—regret—loss? A little of all of them, she supposed. But mostly that a part of her life was over. A chapter closed. No use looking back.

Taking a deep breath, she began to hunt in the bookcase for the copy of the magazine in which she had found the advertisement. She must find another job now—and quick!

CHAPTER TWO

SHE was awakened by the sound of the telephone ringing. Slowly, she dragged herself out of the mists of sleep and swung her feet out of bed. In the hall she snatched up the receiver and held it to her ear, pushing back her hair with her free hand.

'Hello.' Her voice was heavy with slumber.

'Miss Forrest?'

'Mmm——' she smothered a yawn. What time *was* it anyway?

'It's Adam Blake here. I hope I didn't get you out of bed.'

Her eyes were wide open now. 'What? Oh, no, I've been up for hours,' she lied.

'Really? You're an early riser, it's only just on half past seven now!'

She could almost see those supercilious eyebrows rising and she bit her lip. Trust her to say a stupid thing like that! 'And to what do I owe the honour of this early call, Doctor?' she asked a little too sharply.

'Well, actually I'm ringing to offer you the job you applied for yesterday,' he said calmly.

Leane blinked. Had she heard correctly? 'The—the job?' she echoed.

'Yes. Frankly, Miss Forrest, you were the only suitable candidate I interviewed, and as the time is getting short—No doubt you would like to have more details before you decide. It may not be the kind of work you would wish to undertake. I thought we might meet again.'

'You mean you'd like a further interview?' Leane asked.

'I'd prefer to call it an informal talk—perhaps over dinner this evening. Would you be free?'

Leane took a deep breath. 'Is that really necessary? Couldn't you just give me the details now, over the phone?'

'No. I'm sorry, but they're far too confidential.' His tone was tetchy again. 'Well—can you come or not, Miss Forrest? If you've lost interest in the job, you have only to say.'

Leane thought rapidly. Her talk with Tony last night—the way life seemed to have come to a halt for her—her need for a change. Switzerland, a country she had never visited.

'Oh, I'm still interested, Doctor,' she said quickly. 'It was only that——'

'Fine. I'll book a table at the Winchester for eight-thirty. Please try to be on time, Miss Forrest.' And before she could reply he had rung off.

She wandered into the kitchen and put the kettle on. Now that she was up she might as well make a start on the breakfast. Bridget was always ravenous when she came off duty.

She didn't know quite what to make of Adam Blake's call, and she began to wonder suspiciously what could be so confidential about the details of the job. Was the woman some sort of invalid needing special care? Perhaps she was crippled—or blind. But neither of those things would need such secrecy—and as for it not being the kind of work she would care to undertake, he knew she was a qualified nurse and used to those things.

Then a thought occurred to her—Could it possibly be a terminal case? After what she had told him about her distress at losing a patient, he might feel she would have misgivings at the thought of taking on such a case.

She was still musing when Bridget came in, slamming the door behind her with characteristic abandon. She threw open the kitchen door and sniffed appreciatively.

'Mmm—bacon! You're an angel, Lee. I don't know what I'll do without you when you've gone.' She pulled off her cap, releasing the mass of auburn curls. 'My feet are killing me—just going to change—be with you in a minute.' She put her head round the door again. 'Don't forget the baked beans, love. I could eat a bucket of them!'

Leane chuckled to herself as she opened the tin. It was her guess that when she had gone Bridget's staple diet would be baked beans. Over breakfast she told Bridget about the telephone call and her dinner date for this evening. The other girl whistled her approval.

'He's not mean, I'll say that for him! Dinner at the Winchester should put him back a bit. What'll you wear?'

'I haven't had time to think about it yet,' Leane said. 'I've been more concerned about what it is he has to tell me about the job. I've a nasty idea there are some whopping great snags to it.'

'I wouldn't worry about them till you meet them,' Bridget retorted as she slid another slice of bread into the toaster. 'Now—dinner at the Winchester means one of two things, if you ask me: either he fancies you madly or, as you say, he has something to tell you that must be broken gently. But however you look at it, you'll be getting a free dinner!'

Leane laughed. 'I suppose that's one way of looking at it. But of the two things it *has* to be the latter, I can promise you that!' The smile suddenly vanished from her face as she remembered something. 'Oh, by the way, I had a visit from Tony last night after you'd gone. It's all over between us. Why didn't you tell me what was going on, Bridget? It seems it's been all over the hospital.'

Bridget dropped her knife with a clatter and looked up, her usually bright face dismayed. 'Oh Lord! It's true then? I kept hoping it was just gossip. I'm sorry, love, really. I think Tony's a two-timing devil. I mean, the boss's daughter! How low can you stoop?'

Leane shrugged. 'He says it's not like that and I believe him. Anyway, it's not as though we were engaged or anything.'

Bridget blew out her breath explosively. 'You'd been going steady for absolutely *years*! Everyone knows Tony's ambitious, Lee, don't kid yourself. I think you're well rid of him, personally.' She stopped as Leane's eyes filled with sudden tears. 'Oh don't, love. You'll meet someone much nicer—you'll see.'

She went round the table to comfort Leane, but her sympathy only made things worse. When she thought of leaving behind her friend as well as the life she had grown used to, Leane felt bleak. She had an idea that if she were to have dealings with Adam Blake she was going to need a shoulder to cry on.

She took a long time deciding what to wear for the dinner date. She must not look too frivolous or festive, she told herself; yet for the Winchester one couldn't be too casual. What would Adam Blake wear? she wondered and guessed he would be the type to plump for a dark lounge suit. After all, it was a business dinner.

She finally chose a simple black dress, the most expensive one in her wardrobe and one which she had worn only once before, when a friend of Tony's asked them to his engagement party. It had a clinging bodice with a deep V neck and the short sleeves and skirt flared out in a mass of tiny pleats. With it she wore a gold pendant set with a tiny diamond given to her by her aunt on her twenty-first birthday a year ago. When she emerged from the bedroom Bridget whistled.

'Wow! You'll knock his eye out with that! Honestly, you look lovely, Lee. You know, you should wear your hair loose like that all the time. It suits you.'

Bridget was right. Leane's soft brown hair, which she usually wore pinned back into a chignon, made the perfect frame for her small, heart-shaped face and large expressive hazel eyes. She smiled as she looked into the mirror and sighed a little regretfully.

'Goodbye to the nurse image. I've worn my hair like that for so long I'd forgotten there was any other style.'

Bridget was quick to notice the wistful tone in her friend's voice and she said softly: 'Maybe it was time you reassessed yourself and your life,

Lee. You might learn a lot about yourself. After all, you were pretty young when you came into nursing.'

Her face broke into a smile again, dimpling mischievously. 'Who cares about the nurse image, anyway—except perhaps the patients? And there won't be any of them at the Winchester tonight. Off you go and enjoy yourself child!' She looked down at her uniform and pulled a comic face. 'I know one thing—I'd soon change places with you if you asked me to.'

She whisked out of the door and Leane wondered if Bridget really would change places with her, given the choice. She doubted it. Who in their right mind would give up a job she loved and step out into the unknown as she was doing, leaving behind all that was dear and familiar?

She permitted herself the luxury of a cab to the Winchester, and when she arrived she found Adam Blake waiting for her in the foyer. He wore, as she had foreseen, a dark grey lounge suit with a white shirt and sober tie, and he looked handsome but unsmiling as he came towards her.

'Eight-thirty precisely,' he said, looking at his watch. 'I'm glad you're punctual, Miss Forrest.'

An involuntary smile crossed her lips as Bridget's words suddenly came to her mind—'Pompous twit.'

He raised an eyebrow at her. 'Have I said something amusing?'

She looked up at him, the smile quite gone. 'Oh no, Dr Blake, I'm sure you'd never do that.'

He chose to ignore the taunt and put a hand under her elbow. 'Shall we go straight in, or would you like a drink first?'

She was about to suggest that they should go straight into the restaurant when something stopped her. It was a long time since she had been taken out to dine in style. Bridget had advised her to enjoy herself. Why shouldn't she?

'A glass of sherry would be very nice,' she said, smiling up at him.

In the small bar adjoining the restaurant he seemed to relax a little and after the first appreciative sip of her sherry, Leane asked: 'What were the confidential details you wanted to explain to me?'

He took a deep breath and put down his glass. 'First, I must ask you not to let anything that passes between us go any further, Miss Forrest. If you decide not to accept the job—or even if you do.'

Her eyes widened. 'Of course. I believe that, as a nurse, I'm capable of keeping a confidence.'

He nodded, then asked a question that surprised her:

'May I ask how old you are?' He saw her obvious surprise and added quickly: 'It *is* relevant, as you will see in a moment.'

'Almost twenty-two,' she told him.

'Are you a theatre-goer at all?'

She nodded. 'When I have the time—and the money.' She was more puzzled than ever now. But his next question cleared up the other two.

'In that case it's just possible that you remember Romaine Hart. Does the name ring a bell?'

Leane considered. She had been a theatre fan since childhood. The aunt who had brought her up had taken her along with her as often as she could. She was a positive addict and kept scrapbooks containing photographs and press-cuttings of all her favourites. Faintly, Leane recalled a tall, slim blonde with a delicate flowerlike face and beautiful, graceful movement. 'Yes,' she said slowly. 'I seem to remember she played in romantic comedy parts.'

He smiled. 'That's right. How clever of you to remember. It's a good many years now since she played in the West End.'

She looked at him, waiting for him to continue and he cleared his throat. 'Romaine Hart is—would be—your patient, Miss Forrest,' he said quietly.

She stared at him and was about to say something when a waiter appeared at Adam Blake's elbow with the menu. They each made their choice and after the man had gone away, Leane exclaimed:

'It would be thrilling to meet her, of course, but what is the nature of her illness?'

He swallowed the last of his Martini before replying. 'Miss Hart is hoping to make a comeback on the West End stage next year,' he said. 'As I've already mentioned, it's some time since the public last saw her, and she's anxious to make as favourable an impression as possible. Therefore, before she begins rehearsals for a new play, she intends to undergo facial cosmetic surgery.'

She looked at him. 'A face-lift? I wouldn't have thought she was all that old.'

He coloured slightly. 'She isn't old—not old at all! And in my opinion the operation is entirely unnecessary. But actresses are delicate, sensitive creatures and it seems there is a good psychological reason for the operation. Her confidence will be boosted by it. Making a comeback takes a great deal of courage.'

'I can well imagine,' Leane agreed. 'How long has Miss Hart been your patient, Dr Blake?'

He looked startled. 'She's not my patient.'

She was puzzled. 'But you said——'

'That I was her medical adviser,' he supplied. 'I meant informally—as a friend only. Romaine and I have been friends for a long time, and as she has a morbid fear of doctors in their professional capacity she often asks my advice.'

She raised her eyebrows at him. 'And you give it?'

'I do—and it's usually the same advice—to go along to her own G.P. Two years ago he diagnosed slight angina when I urged her to go along. For this reason her operation will be performed under a local anaesthetic.'

Leane winced. 'If she has a fear of medical treatment that will take some courage too.'

He nodded. 'It will—and that's where you come in, Miss Forrest. The surgeon who is to do the operation is an old and trusted friend of Miss Hart's, so that will obviously help.'

Leane smiled wryly. 'For a woman with a morbid fear of doctors she seems to number a few among her friends,' she said.

His brows drew together. 'Only the two of us—myself and Dr Otto Kleber,' he told her. 'And in actual fact neither of us had become doctors when she first knew us.'

'I see.' She lowered her eyes, wondering why he was so touchy on the subject. 'I believe I've heard of Dr Kleber,' she went on, changing the subject. 'Doesn't he have quite a famous clinic in Switzerland? I seem to have read about him from time to time.'

Adam Blake nodded. 'He's done wonderful work in the field of plastic surgery. He also has an after-care clinic and a health-farm high in the mountains near Zurich.'

The waiter came at that moment to tell them that their table was ready, and as Leane followed him through to the restaurant she thought over what Adam Blake had just told her. Life with a once-famous actress at a health farm high in the Swiss mountains would be a far cry from the East End of London and St Ann's—a *very* far cry!

Over the food she asked the questions that had begun to pour into her mind. What would her duties be? If Romaine Hart hated anything medical she wouldn't want the more obvious ministrations of a nurse. Adam Blake was in complete agreement with this last.

'She wouldn't want you to wear a uniform. That goes without saying,' he said. 'Romaine loves beauty and elegance around her. She hates ugliness. I think I told you yesterday that she had asked me to choose someone attractive and lively—she'll expect you to be an amusing and cheerful companion, and to help her entertain any visitors she might have.'

'And still keep a professional eye on her at the same time?' Leane finished for him.

He nodded. 'That's it in a nutshell. Well, Miss Forrest, what do you think?'

She smiled brightly. She felt quite pleasantly relaxed after the sherry and the wine they were drinking with their meal.

'It sounds great!' she said enthusiastically. 'I'll bet a summer in Switzerland beats Hackney any time!'

He looked up at her sharply. 'I must remind you that although the salary is generous and the job may sound cushy, it will not be some kind of rest-cure.'

She felt herself blushing. 'I'm not looking for a cushy job, Dr Blake. I didn't go into nursing expecting a bed of roses.'

His eyes blazed back into hers. 'You didn't stand up to the pressures very well either, did you?' he countered.

She caught her breath. If he had slapped her he couldn't have stung her more. 'If you fear that I may prove unreliable, why are you offering me the job?' she asked, her voice trembling.

'I've told you—because you were the only suitable candidate and the time is short,' he snapped. 'It was Miss Hart's wish to have someone attractive, not mine. If *I* had been choosing a nurse for her——'

'I can imagine!' Leane interrupted. 'You needn't go into details.' She attacked her food with renewed vigour, but after a moment she realised that he was looking at her. She raised an enquiring eyebrow at him.

'Well, Miss Forrest—am I to take it that you are still interested in the job?' he asked.

She laid down her knife and fork very carefully. 'At the risk of appearing flippant, avaricious and lacking in dedication, yes, Doctor—I am still interested.'

He nodded, ignoring her sarcasm. 'Very well.

I've been instructed to invite you down to Miss Hart's home in Hampshire for the weekend—so that you can get to know each other. Will you be free this coming weekend?'

Leane nodded. 'I take it that this is to be a kind of probationary meeting?'

'Naturally, though I think you will enjoy yourself. Romaine has horses, so if you ride you might like to take your things with you. She also likes her guests to dress for dinner in the evenings. As I said, Romaine loves beauty and elegance. You might care to bear that in mind.'

His eyes flickered over her and she said crisply: 'Perhaps you would like to give me some fashion hints Doctor?'

He frowned. 'Not at all, I'm sure you don't need any. On both of our meetings you have looked very—presentable.'

She bowed her head with a hint of exaggeration. 'Thank you, Doctor. You're too kind.'

'Oh—one more thing—Romaine hates formality,' he told her. 'She likes to call everyone by their Christian name. So if you wouldn't mind—in her presence—my name is Adam. Yours, I believe, is Leane?'

She smiled. 'Lee to my friends.'

He wrote Romaine Hart's address on the back of one of his cards and passed it across the table to her. 'It's about two miles out of a village called Gibbet's Cross in the New Forest. I'm afraid it's not easy to get to by train. Have you a car?'

She gave him a wry smile. 'When the rent is paid and the food bought, Doctor, there isn't much left for luxuries on a nurse's salary.'

He gave a curt nod. 'In that case you'd better take

a single ticket to Bournemouth and catch the bus from there. I shan't be able to get there myself until Saturday evening, but I shall be able to give you a lift back to London on Monday morning.'

He went on to give her the directions which she wrote down in her diary over coffee, but as she put down her cup he said:

'I feel I should warn you again that though the job may sound easy, pleasant and lucrative, you may find it quite hard. Romaine is not always an easy person to live with. She has always been used to having things her own way—and under this coming strain——' he shrugged, obviously not wanting to sound disloyal.

Leane felt her irritation rise again. She wished she had never told him about the patient who had died. He obviously thought her a weak person looking for an easy job.

'You need have no fear, Doctor,' she said stiffly. 'I promise you I won't collapse under the pressure.'

He rose from the table. 'I have my car in the hotel car park. Can I give you a lift home?'

She shook her head. 'There is no need to trouble. I shall be quite all right.'

He came round the table and took her arm, looking down at her. 'Please try not to take offence at everything I say, Miss Forrest. And I'd prefer it if you allowed me to see you home. After all, I asked you to come here tonight.'

His car turned out to be an elderly, aristocratic sports model, much restored and, Leane guessed, loved and fussed over. She was right. When she made an admiring remark about it he was obviously pleased.

'She is a beauty, isn't she?' he said. 'She belonged to a friend of mine from my medical school days. I'd always coveted her, and when he bought himself a new Rover last year he sold Perdita to me.'

She laughed. 'Perdita—is that her name?'

'It is, though don't ask me why. I think even Tim, my friend, has forgotten by now. He'd let her go quite shamefully, but I've put in a lot of work on her.' He patted the steering wheel affectionately.

She glanced at his profile. When he smiled he was quite a different person. The dark eyes crinkled attractively at the corners, the mouth and jawline softened. The result was quite arresting. Feeling her eyes on him he turned as they stopped at some traffic lights.

'Do you like cars?'

'I like things that make people come alive,' she said pointedly.

His eyes lingered on hers for a long moment until the hooting of a car behind told him that the lights had changed and he let in the clutch and drew away.

Outside the crumbling Regency terrace, a small part of which was Leane's flat he drew into the kerb. Leane turned to him. 'Thank you for the dinner—and for the lift. Would you like to come in for some more coffee?'

He shook his head. 'I can't park on double yellow lines. I'd hate to see poor Perdita being towed away. Anyway, I have another appointment. I'll see you on Saturday—Miss Forrest.'

'Goodnight—Doctor.' She got out of the car, reflecting that he obviously didn't intend them to be on Christian name terms out of Miss Hart's presence. He had made that plain by the slight emphasis he put on the 'Miss Forrest'. She turned when she got to the top of the steps but the car had moved swiftly back into the stream of traffic and was now lost to her view.

She fumbled in her bag for her key. So that was hurdle number two over. All that remained now was to win the approval of Romaine Hart herself. As she climbed the stairs she wondered ruefully if it would be more difficult to win than that of Adam Blake.

That night she had difficulty in sleeping. She tossed and turned, watching the luminous hands of the alarm clock pass two and three before she finally slipped into oblivion. Once she had got up to heat milk at the kitchen stove, and as she sat drinking it she had thought over her evening with Adam Blake. If only he wasn't so suspicious—so disapproving. She wondered why Romaine Hart had chosen him to do her interviewing for her. He had conducted the whole thing as though it were against his better judgment. It was very strange. Still, once she and Romaine Hart had met they would each know whether he had been right or not.

She pulled a wry face at herself in the kitchen mirror. 'A good thing Dr Adam Blake isn't accompanying us to Switzerland,' she told her reflection. 'I doubt if I could stand three months of his patronising, chauvinistic manner!'

It was hardly surprising that she overslept in the morning, and Bridget woke her with a cup of tea and a reproving look.

'Come on, lazy! You're falling down on your

job as my housekeeper.' She threw herself down heavily across Leane's feet with a sigh. 'What a night! We had two emergency appendectomies and a nasty accident case—all while *you* were out on the town!' She peered at Leane, who was sleepily sipping her tea. 'Well, come on then—tell me all about it. Some of us have to get our pleasure second-hand, you know!'

Leane laughed; Bridget was never short of dates on her evenings off. She put down her cup. 'Well, to begin with, it wasn't like you make it sound at all. Dr Blake was formality itself. The job is mine, subject to the approval of the lady I'm to work for. I'm to go down to the New Forest this weekend to meet her. It'll depend on whether we hit it off or not really, I suppose.'

Bridget wrinkled her nose. 'Where in the New Forest?'

'Just outside a village called Gibbet's Cross,' Leane told her.

She gave a mock shudder. 'Sounds like something out of a horror film! I can just see it—bats flying out from under the eaves—doors creaking. Your old lady will be an aged crone who dabbles in witchcraft. Where did you say she was going for this operation—Transylvania? I'll bet it's a fang transplant!'

Helpless with laughter, Leane threw a pillow at her. 'Oh—go and have your bath while I start the breakfast. Then you can go to bed and give that oversized imagination of yours a rest!'

A little later as she stood at the cooker frying bacon and the inevitable baked beans, she wondered what Bridget would make of the truth if she knew it!

CHAPTER THREE

THE bus rambled lazily through the sleepy afternoon, making frequent stops. It seemed a very long time since they had left Bournemouth but Leane didn't mind at all. She had never been to the New Forest before and she was enthralled. Between the pretty villages were great expanses of open heathland that surprised her. These spaces must once have been covered by trees, she told herself, until the Industrial Revolution had taken its toll of them. Now the peaty land rolled into the distance, covered with heather and gorse that was just beginning to break into purple and gold. Here and there, Leane glimpsed little groups of ponies with tiny new foals, adorable and woolly. She was so delighted and fascinated that she had almost forgotten the reason for her visit when the bus stopped and the conductor called out, 'Gibbet's Cross!'

Leane gathered up her things quickly. She knew she must get off here: Adam Blake had told her that Romaine Hart's house was not on the bus route. As the bus drew away she put down her case and opened her bag to look again at the directions she had jotted down in her diary. But while she was still turning the pages a car drew up alongside her. A tall young man got out and came round the bonnet, smiling at her.

'Would you be Miss Leane Forrest, by any chance?'

She looked up in surprise. 'Yes.'

The man held out his hand. 'I'm Keith Sands. I'm a friend of Romaine's. She asked me to meet you.'

'That's very kind of you. But how did you know which bus to meet?' Leane asked.

He grinned. 'It wasn't difficult to work out. Romaine knew you couldn't be here till afternoon, and the buses only run every hour.'

Leane bit her lip. 'If I'd known I could have telephoned. I was going to walk.'

He picked up her case. 'Never mind. As it happens my first guess was right, but it wouldn't have mattered if it hadn't been. One of my favourite occupations is loafing around!'

He opened the car door for her and she settled into the passenger seat of the sleek, misty grey Jaguar.

'What a lovely car,' she said appreciatively.

He smiled. 'One of my many indulgences, and terribly expensive to run, I'm afraid.' He grinned at her as he switched on the ignition. 'The trouble with extravagances is that they quickly become necessities. Don't you find that?'

Leane smiled wryly. 'That's one problem I *don't* have.' She looked out of the window. 'This is beautiful countryside. I've never been to the New Forest before. Do you live here?'

He shook his head. 'I'm purely a weekend countryman. I have a cottage quite near to where Romaine lives. I try to come down as often as I can.' He turned to smile at her. 'Though I must say that some weekends are definitely more interesting than others!'

She stole a glance at his profile as he turned his

eyes again to the road. He was not handsome, but certainly attractive with his twinkling grey eyes and wide, humorous mouth.

They were driving uphill now, away from the village. There were tall trees on either side of them but as they reached the top of the hill the trees came to an abrupt end revealing a rolling panorama of heathland studded with young trees and clumps of bushes. Beneath the blue of the sky the colours were dazzling. As they came to a crossroads Keith Sands turned to her.

'This is where the gibbet used to stand,' he told her. 'That's where the village goot its name.'

He nodded to where a stone plaque was set into the close-cropped grass at the side of the road. 'That stone marks the spot.' He gazed out over the wind-swept heath. 'You can just imagine the felons' bodies swaying in the wind, can't you?' He chuckled at her shudder. 'Well, they had to do something to deter the highwaymen, didn't they?'

'Highwaymen? How interesting!' Leane exclaimed.

He nodded. 'Oh yes, a favourite place for them, this was. Well, you can imagine, can't you? Plenty of cover. They have it that this place iss haunted——' He broke off to grin sheepishly. 'Maybe I should explain that I'm a writer. That's why I'm so interested in local history, though I don't write it. My line is comedy.'

She laughed. 'I'm relieved to hear it!'

They turned right at the crossroads, then, about half a mile further on another right turn, nosing the car down a leafy narrow lane, thick with rhododendrons which grew in profusion on either side, their buds just beginning to show the crimson and purple promise of what was to come. Presently they came to a white-painted gate with a cattle grid in front of it. Keith turned the car into the opening.

'Welcome to Heathridge House,' he said as he got out to open the gate.

The long drive was lined with more rhododendrons and azaleas, but when it opened out into the circular sweep in front of the house, Leane gasped with delight. Built in mock-Tudor style with black-beamed walls, the house seemed to bask in its idyllic surroundings. The roof was a mellow rose-red and the lattice windows winked in the sunlight. As Keith drew the car to a halt before the studded oak door, a plump, smiling woman came out to meet them.

'Good afternoon, Miss. I'm Edna Baker, Miss Hart's housekeeper. I'm glad Mr Sands was able to meet you. My Stan would've come, but he had to take one of the horses to the blacksmith. Miss Hart's out riding at the moment, but I'm expecting her back at any minute. Will you come this way?'

Keith carried Leane's case into the hall. 'Well, there you are, then, safely delivered.'

Leane smiled. 'Perhaps I'll see you again.'

'I'm afraid you will. I'm invited for dinner on Sunday, and now that I know you're here I wouldn't miss it for the world!' He grinned wickedly at her. 'Be good.'

The room to which Edna Baker showed Leane was at the back of the house and overlooked the garden. Curtains with pink roses hung at the windows and there was a rose-shaded lamp by the bed. Leane looked out of the window at the sunlit lawn.

'It's lovely, Mrs Baker. Thank you.'

The woman smiled. 'Call me Edna, love. Everyone does.'

After she had washed and changed, Leane unpacked her case. As she took out her jodhpurs and riding hat she looked at them ruefully. It was at least two years since she had ridden, and she wondered if she could remember how. She would hate to fall off and make a fool of herself.

She went downstairs and into the large room overlooking the garden, as Edna had instructed. A moment later the tinkle of teacups heralded the arrival of Edna wheeling a laden trolley.

'Madam's just come in,' she said. 'She's just gone up to tidy herself, she'll be down in a jiffy. Would you like a cup of tea now?'

Leane shook her head. 'No, I'll wait, thank you.'

Mrs Baker withdrew and Leane went over to the fireplace where a cheerful log fire burned. She did not hear anyone enter the room and when the soft, musical voice addressed her she spun round, startled.

'Good afternoon—oh, I'm sorry, did I make you jump?'

'Oh, no, not at all.' Leane found herself looking into the only pair of true violet eyes she had ever seen. She held out her hand. 'I'm Leane Forrest. It was good of you to invite me.'

'I'm Romaine Hart, and it was good of you to come all this way.'

The hand that held hers was white and cool

with delicately shaped and varnished nails, and Leane was surprised to see that her face was as fragile and flower-like as she remembered it; the hair, worn in a halo of blonde curls, as glossy as ever.

She smiled. 'I'm so pleased to meet you, Miss Hart. I saw a good many of your plays before your retirement from the stage.'

Romaine smiled radiantly. 'So Adam told me. I was quite convinced that everyone had forgotten me, especially people of your generation. It was very heartening for me to find someone who remembered.'

She turned to the trolley and began to pour the tea. In the simple white shirt and jodhpurs she was as slim and straight as a reed, and Leane wondered why on earth she felt the need of cosmetic surgery. On a stage, with make-up she would easily pass for under thirty still, although, doing a rapid sum, Leane worked out her age at nearer to fifty.

Romaine turned and handed her a cup of tea and a plate. 'Do help yourself—I hope Adam told you that I love to be informal. I'd like you to call me Romaine. I shall call you Leane, a charming name.'

Leane opened her handbag. 'I was looking through my souvenir box last night and I found some programmes I'd kept of plays I'd particularly enjoyed. Some were yours.' She held out two programmes. 'Look, these two have photographs.'

Romaine took them and looked at them with a wistful little sigh. 'Ah, such happy days. I wonder if they'll ever come again? Youth is gone before you have time to appreciate it.'

Leane took her courage in both hands. 'If I may say so, I don't think that is so in your case.'

Romaine smiled, touching the skin around her eyes. 'I wish you were right, but my mirror tells me otherwise. I can't close my eyes any longer to the lines and the little pouches.' She pulled off the wisp of silk she wore round her throat. 'Here too. My dear, if I don't do something quickly I shall be a withered old lady.'

Leane laughed. 'That's absurd. Anyway, I often think people grow more attractive with maturity. Their faces gain character.'

But Romaine held up her hands in horror. 'I want to make a comeback, my dear. I was never what you would call a brilliant actress. I must do what I'm good at—and that's romantic comedy.'

Leane saw her point. Even though she herself considered an operation unnecessary, Romaine would obviously gain a great deal of confidence from it. And who was she to argue with that?

Romaine put down her cup and leaned forward. 'Tell me, how do you get along with Adam?'

'Oh—very well,' Leane said guardedly.

'That's good. He was certainly very enthusiastic about you,' Romaine told her. 'Whoever I employ must always fit in with the other members of my household. I couldn't bear to have people quarrelling around me.' She smiled. 'Edna seems to have taken to you too, which is fortunate because she and her husband Stan will be accompanying us to Switzerland.'

Leane felt pleased. She had sensed a kindred spirit in Edna Baker.

'After the operation,' Romaine was saying, 'I may invite some author friends over. I hope to be reading some plays. As you're a keen theatregoer you might like to help me. You see, I still have to choose the play in which I shall make my return to the stage and as you can imagine, it's a very important choice.' She lay back in her chair and half closed her eyes. 'I can't make up my mind between a revival and a completely new play.'

'Something in costume would be nice,' Leane suggested. 'A Restoration comedy, perhaps.'

Romaine opened her eyes and gave her a brilliant smile. 'What a wonderful idea! I must put it to my agent. I have a new one and he'll be coming to dinner on Sunday evening. I've invited a few people. I thought it might make it less dull for you.' She sighed. 'I'm afraid I've grown very boring, languishing here in the country. Adam is always nagging at me to make more of a social life for myself.'

She smiled. 'I've never needed crowds of chattering people though. One or two dear friends of whom I'm fond was always enough for me. That's why it will be so important to have them with me in Switzerland.'

An uncomfortable suspicion had begun to grow in Leane's mind. 'But surely,' she said hesitantly, 'Dr Blake will not be able to leave his practice.'

Romaine's eyebrows rose. 'Oh, didn't he tell you? He's Registrar at Great Horton Street Hospital, and he's taking three months' leave.'

Leane stared at her. 'To accompany you, you mean?'

Romaine smiled, her head on one side. 'Yes

and no. He's always wanted to specialise in plastic surgery and this is a wonderful opportunity for him to study the work of a famous man. Dr Otto Kleber is another very old friend of mine, and he's agreed to let Adam study with him whilst I'm there.'

Leane was both shocked and surprised. He had seemed to have such strong feelings on the subject of loyalty and priorities, and yet here he was allowing this wealthy woman friend to finance a course of study for him. She thought furiously about the way he had preached at her about leaving St Ann's. In addition, he would be there with them in Switzerland for the whole three months! She was quite appalled by the thought.

'Is something wrong?' Romaine was looking at her curiously.

'No.' She quickly resumed her smile. 'It was just that Dr Blake didn't mention that he was going to Switzerland too.'

Romaine smiled. 'I have to confess that my motives are not entirely unselfish. I rather fancied the thought of having Adam with me.'

Leane cleared her throat. What exactly was the relationship between these two? 'I'm sure you'll be wanting to hear about my qualifications,' she said, but Romaine waved a graceful white hand at her.

'Oh no, I'm sure Adam has satisfied himself on that score.' She smiled. 'I'm a bit of an ostrich, my dear. All I want is for you and me to be good friends. The fact that you are a nurse will obviously be invaluable, but I prefer to think of you more as a companion—just as I do Adam.'

So that was it! Leane couldn't help smiling to herself. To surround oneself with well qualified medical 'friends' at such a time seemed like a very wise move indeed! Even though, in Romaine's case, it must prove expensive.

Romaine stood up. 'If you've finished your tea perhaps you'd like to come and see my horses. Do you ride?'

Leane nodded. 'I used to. I must be terribly rusty now though.'

'My darlings are as gentle as lambs,' Romaine told her. 'I'm sure you'll be safe enough with them.'

The stables were behind the garage and housed three horses: a gentle white mare, a bay gelding and a big aristocratic-looking roan with a white star on his forehead. Romaine introduced them each in turn.

'This is Kate.' She stroked the mare's velvet nose affectionately. 'My super-dainty Kate. The prettiest Kate in Christendom.' She laughed. 'And if she ever was a shrew she was tamed before she came to me!' She moved on to the gelding. 'This is Brutus. Adam likes him and always rides him when he comes down, otherwise Stan exercises him every morning. And this beauty—' she pointed to the roan—'is Malvolio, because he has delusions of grandeur, bless his heart.'

'All names from Shakespeare,' Leane smiled.

'Yes, isn't it fun? Take any of them you like while you're here, my dear. A girl from the village comes in to look after them each day and she's usually here to saddle up for you. You may like a gallop before breakfast—great for toning up the liver.' She laughed. 'Though I'm sure your liver doesn't need any toning up!'

Throughout dinner Romaine talked, drawing out Leane and finding out all that they had in common. As well as a love of the theatre they found that they both appreciated beautiful scenery, and Romaine bubbled with delight when she discovered that Leane had never visited Switzerland before.

'Oh, my dear, you have *such* a treat in store,' she said. 'And to think that I shall be the one to show it to you! Mavos is the most beautiful place on earth, I'm convinced of it. Such richness! The brilliant colours. It seems almost unreal. I am renting a lovely chalet high in the mountains, quite close to Otto's clinic, so that if all goes well I shall be able to come home the day after the operation—with you to look after me and Otto visiting every day, of course. The little town is quite out of this world; nestling in the valley. All the mountain springs run down to the lake in summer so that everywhere you go there is the cool sound of running water.' She smiled ecstatically. 'But I shan't tell you too much about it or it won't be a surprise.'

'It sounds wonderful. I can hardly wait,' Leane said. 'If you're quite sure I'm really the sort of person you're looking for.'

Romaine patted her hand. 'There isn't any doubt in my mind about that, dear. I knew I could trust Adam to choose just the right girl for me. He has such good taste in women—and of course he knows a good nurse when he sees one. I'm sure the three of us are going to get along just famously.'

Later that night, as Leane lay in the rose-coloured bedroom she wondered if Romaine's confidence could be justified. Adam Blake had not chosen her for her qualities as a nurse. He obviously derided those. He didn't appear to like her much as a woman either. She would just have to hope that the chalet in Mavos was big enough for them to stay out of each other's way as much as possible.

She woke early. Looking at her watch she found that it was barely six o'clock, yet she felt wide awake. She got up and stood looking down into the garden bathed in early light and pearled with dew. Should she go for a walk? Then she thought of the horses. It would be a good opportunity to take her first ride unobserved, and it was a perfect morning for a canter on the heath.

She dressed quickly, putting on her jodhpurs and a thick yellow polo sweater, then, her riding hat in her hand, she went quietly down the stairs.

The girl from the village Romaine had spoken of had obviously been in, the loose boxes were open at the top and two of the three animals were sniffing the morning air appreciatively. The third, Brutus, was missing and Leane guessed that he was being exercised. She looked at the remaining two. She'd better not take Kate, the mare, in case Romaine came to ride her. That left the lofty Malvolio.

She eyed him apprehensively. He was very large, though Romaine had said they were all three gentle. She held out her hand and he nuzzled it, whinnying softly. Well, he seemed friendly enough.

Opening the door cautiously, she led him out of

his loose box, and saddled him without any trouble, then she mounted and walked him out through a gate that led into the rhododendron lined lane. Trotting along in the pleasant, fresh morning air Leane felt alive and tingling. This was wonderful. The 'posting' movement came back to her as though she had ridden only yesterday, and from the lofty height of Malvolio's back she could see the crossroads looming up ahead. Soon she would let him have his head and they would gallop over the heather until she could see what lay on the other side of the rise.

But after they had crossed the main road to the heathland and Leane had loosened the reins and urged her mount forward with her heels, she soon discovered what Romaine had meant when she said Malvolio had 'delusions of grandeur'. Given his head, the horse went like the wind, his ears back and his silky mane flying. He obviously thought he was a racehorse! Leane tried to bring him under control but he would have none of it. Once given his freedom, he was obviously going to make the most of it and work out all his pent-up energy.

Leane hung on like grim death, lying forward over the animal's neck. On he went, his hooves thudding rhythmically on the peaty ground. She could hear the hiss of his breathing mingling with the beating of her own heart as she clung on, her face against his neck. Then, coming to a group of gorse bushes he sprang over them and she cried out in alarm as she felt herself becoming unseated. On went Malvolio, regardless of the plight of his lop-sided rider. Tossing his head joyously, he bounced forward, and Leane felt herself sliding helplessly out of her saddle. Any minute now she would be forced to let go and hit the flying ground that came nearer and nearer to her as she slipped.

She heard the shout just as she was about to let go. Someone was coming to her aid, and at once her strength seemed to return. She heard the thudding of other hooves—someone called Malvolio's name and rode along side to grasp at his bridle. The pace slackened—slowed and finally stopped, and Leane dragged herself into an upright position again and found herself looking into the eyes of Adam Blake.

'Why on earth did you choose to take Malvolio when you are as incompetent as that?' he demanded angrily. 'Of all the stupid things to do. You might have injured him!'

Leane felt her face go scarlet. 'How was I to know he'd go mad like that?' she said indignantly.

'It's you who are mad! A horse always knows when he can play up. Don't you know that?' He dismounted, glaring at her. 'You'd better get off and let me ride him back.' He held the horse's head while she slid unceremoniously to the ground. She felt foolish and dangerously near to tears.

'I *could* have been injured myself, let alone the horse,' she said petulantly, her lip trembling.

He looked at her sharply. 'Are you all right? You do look a bit flushed.' He reached out and took her arm with his free hand but she shook it off.

'I'm perfectly all right, thank you,' she said stiffly. 'And I thought you weren't coming down until tonight.'

'Did you? Well, it's rather fortunate for you that I decided to come sooner, isn't it? Would you rather get up on Brutus? He's worked off his freshness. You won't have any trouble with him.'

She mounted with difficulty, her limbs stiff from Malvolio's rough treatment. 'Thank you,' she said coldly.

He mounted the now quiet horse and regarded her for a moment, his lips twitching. 'You hat's crooked,' he observed. 'And there's a smudge on your nose.'

Furiously she corrected both defects, scrubbing at her nose with one finger. He laughed and turned Malvolio's head.

'You'd better follow me home. I prescribe a hot bath with plenty of salts and then a hearty breakfast. That's if you can open that stiff upper lip far enough to eat it!'

She hated his broad back in its tweed hacking-jacket all the way back to Heathridge House.

CHAPTER FOUR

AFTER her bath, Leane dressed carefully in a cream silk shirt and tweed skirt. She also took special care over her hair and make-up. She had felt at a dreadful disadvantage over the horse incident and she needed the assurance that her appearance at least was dignified when she faced Adam Blake at breakfast.

At the table Adam had Romaine in gales of laughter as he recounted the runaway horse adventure. 'I come down to Gibbet's Cross for a bit of peace and quiet and here I am playing Sir Galahad before I've even had my breakfast!' he said.

Leane made herself laugh with them, but she was furious with him for exploiting her humiliation in this mean way. Romaine need never have known anything about it.

'He's showing off in front of her,' she told herself resentfully. 'He can be pleasant enough when she's around! I wonder what she'd have thought if she'd heard the tone of voice he used to me and the way he called me stupid?'

But in spite of her resentment the bright smile remained firmly glued to her face. If he could play games of make-believe, then so could she. And it looked as though they'd both have plenty of practise!

After breakfast he excused himself and went off to pay some calls, roaring off down the drive in Perdita. After waving him off from the porch, Romaine turned to her and took her arm.

'Isn't he wonderful? It cheers me up so much to have him around.' She smiled at Leane. 'And I'm so glad to see that you and he get along so well together.'

So all that show of good humour was for Romaine's benefit? Leane smiled grimly to herself. For all the teasing banter at the breakfast table no doubt Adam Blake still thought her stupid. He was like a split personality—all sweetness and light for Romaine, all irritable bad temper for her. She thought of the three months' study course he was about to embark on and reflected wryly that he knew on which side his bread was buttered.

'Come and see my rose garden,' Romaine was saying. 'It's my pride and joy. Of course there are no blooms as yet, but I can tell you all about them.'

Even though, as Romaine had said, there were no roses in bloom, Leane could appreciate the beauty of the rose garden. It was circular in shape and sunken, with shallow steps leading into it from the lawn. The beds radiated from a sundial in the centre and there was a little stone bench supported by two stone cupids.

'When all the roses are out one can sit here and bask in their perfume,' Romaine said with a smile. 'I chose them all for their fragrance—except this one.' She touched the leaves of a large bush growing next to the bench. 'This is my favourite, pure white, the Iceberg rose. In the old days, when I appeared in a new play I always filled my dressing-room with them. I've always looked on it as my lucky charm.'

Leane looked at her future employer. With the sun glinting on her fair hair and the violet eyes dreamy with reminiscence, she certainly didn't look a day over thirty. True, she wore one of the wispy scarves around her throat again and her face was expertly made up to hide the small imperfections wrought by time, but her figure in the shirt and slim trousers was like a teenager's, and her movements were as graceful and relaxed as Leane remembered them from the actress's heyday.

Adam did not return for lunch and Romaine said that he had telephoned to say that he would be lunching with a doctor friend who lived on the outskirts of Bournemouth. He must have felt that she would be disappointed, because he had suggested taking her out for dinner at a local Country Club that evening.

'And of course you must come too,' Romaine said.

But Leane shook her head. 'No, I'll be fine here with something on a tray. I'm sure there must be things you want to discuss.'

Romaine frowned. 'Are you sure, my dear? I don't like the idea of leaving you here alone. It seems so inhospitable.'

But Leane sensed that her suggestion was not unwelcome, and she assured Romaine that she would be quite happy. 'I'm really very tired,' she said. 'I find this Hampshire air very relaxing and I was up very early. I'll be pleased to go to bed early with a book.'

It was well after midnight when Leane finally laid down the book she had been reading. It was a biography of a well-known Edwardian actress that she had found among the selection at the bedside, and she had read on, too fascinated in spite of her tiredness to put it down. But after she had switched off the light she found that she was unbearably thirsty.

Slipping out of bed, she crossed the room and listened at the door. The house was quiet. Would she disturb anyone if she went to the bathroom for a glass of water? She put on her dressing gown and went across the landing to fill her glass at the cold tap, then started on the return journey, her bare feet making no sound on the thick carpet. Suddenly a door opened right in front of her and she gasped as she found herself face to face with Adam Blake. For a startled moment they stared at each other, then he gave her a curt nod.

'Goodnight.'

She swallowed hard. 'Goodnight.'

He crossed the landing and went into the room opposite, closing the door firmly. Leane stared at the door of the room he had come out of. It was Romaine's room.

She did not go riding again on Sunday morning, and for most of the day she found herself keeping out of Adam's way. She felt extremely awkward. It seemed obvious to her now that the relationship between Adam and Romaine was a close, intimate one, and though she was to be a necessary member of the party travelling to Switzerland, Adam evidently resented her for this reason. She began to wonder seriously whether she had made the wrong decision in accepting the job.

She dressed carefully for the dinner party that evening, choosing a dress of deep lilac. It was cut on slim lines, the flared skirt swirling gracefully round her legs. As she pirouetted in front of her mirror she wished that she had Romaine's fluid grace of movement to go with it.

The rest of the party was made up of John Wilton, Romaine's agent; Keith Sands, the local doctor and his wife, and a young woman named Sylvia Kendal, whom Romaine introduced as the daughter of the local vicar. As she looked round the room as they took a pre-dinner cocktail, one thing struck Leane forcibly: none of the people present was over thirty. Romaine obviously liked to surround herself with youth. She was learning more about her future employer by the hour!

She felt someone touch her arm and turned to see Keith Sands standing at her side, looking debonair in his evening clothes.

'So we meet again,' he said smiling.

She raised her glass. 'So we do.'

'I hear you're going to Switzerland with Romaine,' he said. 'Lucky girl. I keep angling for an invitation myself, but no luck so far. I've just written a play that would be perfect for Romaine.' He looked at her, his head on one side. 'Going as her secretary, are you?'

Leane bit her lip. Obviously, she couldn't tell the truth. 'Sort of,' she said evasively. 'More of a general dogsbody-cum-companion really.'

He raised an eyebrow. 'I wouldn't have thought she'd need another companion with Adam there.' He shrugged. 'But then I suppose it's always nice for a woman to have another female to talk to.' He bent his head closer. 'How about putting in a good word for me, eh?'

She laughed. 'I'm afraid I don't have that sort of influence. Why don't you ask Dr Blake—Adam?'

He pulled a face. 'I don't think he likes me much. I've a shrewd suspicion that he finds me flippant. One of your "life is real—life is earnest" types, our Adam.'

Edna produced a delicious dinner and afterwards Romaine, who was looking beautiful in a gown of black lace which emphasised her fragile loveliness, insisted on playing records for dancing. She opened the French windows that led on to the terrace and reached for Adam's hand as the romantic strains filled the air. Soon the others followed suit, and Leane found herself in the arms of Keith Sands. He made her laugh a lot with his ready wit, and she found herself relaxing and enjoying herself more than she had done all weekend. She wished rather wistfully that he was to be a member of the Swiss party. He would certainly liven things up.

She was having a conversation with the young doctor and his wife a little later when Adam touched her arm.

'Dance with me, Lee?'

She stared at him in amazement, then turned to the doctor and his wife. 'Will you excuse me?'

With Adam's hand under her elbow she found herself being propelled out through the French windows on to the terrace. There, Adam drew her close and they began to dance. For a moment or two neither of them spoke, then he held her a little away from him and looked down into her eyes.

'You seem to be enjoying yourself.'

'I am—very much,' she said. 'I hope that meets with your approval, Dr Blake.'

'Adam, please,' he said. 'And would you mind telling me why I always get this hostile reaction from you?'

She looked up at him. 'What else do you expect when you so obviously disapprove of practically everything I do?'

He smiled and she was disarmed—reminded of the night he had taken her home in his car and they had talked on an almost friendly basis. He really did look incredibly handsome in his dinner-jacket. The glances Sylvia Kendal had been giving him had not escaped her notice either.

'I think you're rather exaggerating,' he said. 'After all, we hardly know each other yet. I think you dance very well.'

'How very kind of you,' she said with heavy sarcasm.

He frowned. 'If we're going to see a lot of one another—and I don't see how it can be avoided under the circumstances—don't you think we'd better call a truce to this ridiculous verbal duel we seem to have got ourselves into?'

Good food, good company and the wine she had drunk had put Leane into a relaxed mood and she smiled up at him. He was right. It would be a terrible strain, keeping up their feud for the three whole months. 'It is a bit silly, I suppose,' she confessed.

He laughed softly and his arm tightened round her waist as he whisked her away to the far end of the terrace. When they came to the steps leading down to the lawn he stopped dancing and took her hand.

'Shall we walk for a little?'

She nodded hesitantly, wondering what he could have to say to her that needed privacy. They went across the grass and down the steps into the rose garden, walking in silence till he said: 'Well, what do you feel about the job now? About Romaine?'

She smiled. 'I think she's very charming—and I think the job will be interesting.'

'She seems to have taken to you.'

'I'm glad.'

He stopped walking and turned to look at her.

'And how do you feel about me being there? I understand you didn't realise I would be.'

She shrugged, feeling her colour rise. 'Does it matter?'

'Yes, it does.'

He spoke so firmly that she gave him a puzzled look 'Not to you, surely?'

'No—to Romaine.'

For some strange reason the stark honesty of his reply was like a blow in the face, and she turned her head from him.

'Of course, I see. She hates discord and you don't want her to be upset—being so—so close. It's only natural.' She began to walk back in the direction of the house, Adam following her closely.

'Wait!' he demanded angrily. 'What do you mean by that? *Wait* a minute!' He grasped her arm and jerked her roughly to a standstill. For a moment he glared angrily into her eyes, clearly reading what he saw in them.

'Now listen—what you saw—last night——' But she shook her head vigorously, refusing to allow him to finish.

'It's none of my business. I'd prefer not to know,' she said.

'It wasn't what you obviously think,' he said persistently.

'I didn't *think*. It's not what I'm employed for, is it?'

His hand was still on her arm and he shook her gently. 'Why are you so damned stubborn? Listen——'

'I won't listen,' she shouted. 'If it's a condition of my employment that I appear to be friendly with you, then I'll go along with it. But that doesn't mean I have to change my opinion of you!'

'Which is?' He jerked her towards him.

Her heart was beating very fast and she was having trouble with her breathing, but she hated the thought that he might see that he was upsetting her. 'Which—which is—oh, never mind!'

Without warning he caught her to him and kissed her hard, steadying her twisting head with one strong hand. The breath was completely dashed from her body and she felt her knees turn to water. When he drew away from her she saw that his eyes were still burning with fury. Without a word he took her hand and walked quickly up the steps and back across the lawn.

On the terrace he slipped an arm around her waist and drew her once more into the dancing. Out of the corner of her eye she saw Romaine dancing with John Wilton. She smiled happily and waved to them.

Adam rested his cheek against Leane's. His closeness, the sheer masculinity of him took her breath away. Suddenly she felt herself losing control of the situation, she felt vulnerable—helpless. His lips moved against her cheek.

'Look at me,' he whispered.

She moved her head till her eyes met his wonderingly.

'Now *smile*—as though you meant it,' he said between clenched teeth.

So that was it. All this was for Romaine's benefit. But was he trying to show her how well they liked each other—or attempting to make her jealous? Either way she felt she was being used. Just at that moment the music came to an end and she pushed him away.

'I think it's time you circulated,' she said coldly and moved quickly out of his reach. This was one game of make-believe she wasn't prepared to play!

She avoided Adam for the rest of the evening, seeking the company of Keith Sands, whose wit, after several drinks, was sharper than ever. He rendered her almost helpless with laughter with some of his stories of well-known personalities he had written for, and she began to feel that Romaine would be lucky to have such a talent working for her. Once or twice she caught Adam looking in their direction, a frown bringing his heavy brows together, and she couldn't deny the stab of pleasure she got from his obvious disapproval.

It was well after midnight when the last of the guests departed, and after saying goodnight to Romaine, Leane took herself off to bed. As she slipped out of the lilac dress she thought of Keith's parting words. He had asked for her telephone number and suggested that they might meet in London before she flew off to Switzerland.

'I might be able to give you a few tips on how to handle Romaine,' he whispered enigmatically. 'I've a feeling you might need them!'

She wondered vaguely what he had meant, but after she had switched off the bedside lamp and closed her eyes her last involuntary thoughts were of Adam—the firmness of his arms around her and the hard ruthlessness of his lips on hers.

Breakfast was an early, rushed affair as Adam had an appointment in London at eleven-thirty. They took their leave of Romaine who stood on the porch in a floating blue housecoat. Adam threw Leane's case into the back of the car and a moment later they were roaring down the drive. She looked at him out of the corner of her eye, wishing fervently that she had taken the train back to London. If the entire journey were to be spent in silence she didn't know if she could stand the strain.

Feeling her eyes on him, he turned. 'How are you this morning? Have you recovered from the party?'

'I haven't got a hangover, if that's what you mean!'

He made a small explosive snort. 'God! Is there nothing I can say that you won't twist into an insult?'

She shrugged. 'Does it bother you?'

'I have tried, God knows,' he said exasperatedly. 'I bent over backwards last night to be friendly.'

Anger rose in her like a fountain. 'Do you really think I want that sort of thing?' she asked shrilly. 'Did you think that all you had to do to make me fall beneath your fatal charm was to kiss me? Did you think it would automatically erase your previous ill-mannered treatment of me?' She gave a short laugh. 'I'm afraid you either overestimated your own charm or *under*-estimated my intelligence!'

He made no reply, but his white-knuckled grip on the wheel and the grim lines of his mouth spoke of his annoyance. She noted both with satisfaction.

'And while we're on the subject, Dr Blake,' she

went on, 'I applied for this job because I need money with which to support myself and I found myself unable to continue with my job at the hospital. *I* am not fortunate enough to have a benefactress willing to finance expensive sabbaticals for me. I think you had a darned cheek to criticise me under the circumstances.'

The car swerved dangerously and screeched to a halt under some trees. Adam switched off the engine and turned to her, his eyes blazing.

'You certainly have a vicious tongue,' he snapped, his voice ragged with control. 'You can just listen to me now. Never in my life has anyone paid a penny for my education or my training. I've achieved what I have through my own efforts.'

She turned her head away. 'I'm not interested.'

'Well, you're going to damned well hear about it anyway!' He grasped her shoulders and turned her towards him. 'I was brought up by foster-parents and managed to get into the local Grammar school. After A-levels I went to university and then on to Great Horton Street. Plastic surgery has always been the subject closest to my heart and Romaine knew it. So when she decided to have this operation she put a proposition to me: my moral support in return for three months studying Dr Kleber's methods.'

Leane's chin lifted. 'How nice for you.'

'It took a long time and a lot of heart-searching before I decided,' he went on, 'but in the end I decided that I could only be doing good by accepting—to Romaine, to my career and, ultimately, to my future patients.'

She met his eyes and in them saw the sincerity

and the uncertainty he had gone through. She knew in that moment that he was telling the truth and she bit her lip.

'I'm sorry,' she said. 'I shouldn't have burst out at you like that. It's none of my business anyway.'

He let go of her shoulders and relaxed in his seat with a sigh. 'It doesn't matter. I don't know why I let your remarks annoy me so much. You caught me on the raw, I suppose.' He glanced at her. 'You're rather emotional for a nurse, aren't you?' he asked levelly. 'Was that perhaps something to do with your decision to leave?'

She nodded. 'It may have been—partly.'

There was a long silence during which Leane noticed the clearness of the morning air, the birdsong and the spicy fragrance of the pine trees. Adam looked at her.

'I owe you an apology—for last night. I'm afraid I behaved very badly. I promise you it won't happen again.'

He turned the ignition key and as the engine sprang to life Leane's heart sank. Without quite knowing why or how, she felt she had spoilt something.

In the flat Leane crept about, unpacking quietly so as not to wake Bridget. She felt depressed. Things were not going at all as she expected. If only it weren't for Adam Blake, she would be looking forward to the new job. It would be quite an adventure—seeing a new country and experiencing a branch of surgery that fascinated her. She felt sure that she and Romaine Hart could get along together, but whenever she and

Adam were in the same room the sparks began to fly. Her outburst this morning would do nothing to improve their relationship either, she thought. She felt sure that if there were only time enough he would suggest readvertising the job and asking her to step down.

The unpacking done, she took a basket and set out for the shops. One peep into the cupboards told her that they had run out of almost everything—except baked beans! When she got back she found Bridget in the kitchen yawning over the stove as she made coffee. When she saw the laden basket her face brightened.

'Oh Lee, you are an angel! I was going to do that before you got back. I didn't expect you so early.' She sighed and stretched her arms luxuriously. 'Ah—just think: three days off and no more nights for a while. What bliss! Now, I'll tell you what I'm going to do—I'm going to spend my time off giving you the benefit of my sartorial expertise.'

Leane snatched the pan of boiling milk from the stove a second before it boiled over. 'What on earth are you talking about?' she asked.

Bridget groaned. 'No use talking to you, is it? In plain language, I'm going to help you to choose some new clothes. Do you realise that you haven't a thing to wear?'

'And how do you make that out?' Leane asked.

'I had a date on Sunday afternoon and I thought you wouldn't mind if I borrowed something of yours,' Bridget explained. 'Well—when I looked into your wardrobe—dragsville! Not a presentable stitch in sight!'

Leane laughed. 'Poor you! Didn't it occur to

you that I might have taken my clothes away with me for the weekend?'

Bridget took the mug of coffee Leane handed her. 'Well, yes, but a weekend's-worth of decent clobber isn't going to get you far, is it? Not on a three-month trip to Switzerland with a rich lady! You never know—play your cards right and you might land a wealthy husband.'

Leane perched on the kitchen stool and looked thoughtfully at her friend. Ignoring the bit about landing a wealthy husband there was something in what she said. Her doubts crowded in again. 'I'm not at all sure I ought to go,' she responded gloomily.

Bridget sighed. 'Oh dear—like that, was it? Bit of an old tartar, is she?'

'No—quite the opposite. The biggest snag is that Dr Adam Blake—the one who interviewed me—is to be one of the party, and we just don't hit it off.'

'Then just ignore him,' Bridget suggested. 'After all, he's not the boss, is he? If you want to go—*go*!'

Leane sighed. Things always seemed so straightforward to Bridget. 'Well, you're right about the clothes,' she said. 'It's ages since I bought anything new. Maybe a shopping trip will help to take my mind off things.'

They decided to treat themselves to lunch out as well, and spent a thoroughly enjoyable afternoon buying Leane a new summer wardrobe. It was almost six o'clock when they returned from the West End, and when they reached the top of the stairs they could hear the telephone ringing inside.

'Oh, let it ring!' Bridget said, sitting down gratefully on the top step to get her breath back. But Leane was already scrabbling in her bag for the key. She found it, opened the door and snatched up the receiver.

'Hello—Leane Forrest speaking,' she said breathlessly.

'Oh, Leane—Romaine here. I was beginning to think you must be out. I just wanted to satisfy myself that you'd got home safely. That terrible car of Adam's frightens the life out of me.'

Leane smiled. 'How thoughtful of you. We had quite a good journey and arrived in plenty of time, thank you. May I say once more how much I enjoyed my weekend?'

'It was a pleasure having you, dear. I really can't tell you how pleased I am that Adam chose you, Leane,' she said. 'I feel we have a real rapport. I'll tell you a little secret: I was just a tiny bit afraid of this operation, but now that I know I'll have you with me, my fears are completely laid to rest.'

Leane was rather taken aback. 'It's very kind of you to say so.'

'Not kind at all. I'll let you know the time of our flight as soon as I know it, Leane,' Romaine went on. 'All you have to do is to make sure your passport is in order. I shall look forward to seeing you at the airport on the twenty-sixth. Goodbye, dear.'

'Goodbye, and thanks again.' Leane put the receiver down and turned to Bridget who had come inside and was leaning against the doorjamb.

'Needn't tell me. I heard,' she said. 'Knowing you, I suppose that will have made you feel indispensable.'

Leane nodded. Her boats appeared to have been well and truly burned.

They had just finished eating their tea when the telephone rang again. Bridget answered it and came back into the room a moment later with a twinkle in her eye.

'For you again—a guy who calls himself Keith Sands.'

Leane went into the tiny hall and picked up the receiver.

'Hello, Keith.'

'I wondered if you were busy this evening, Lee.' Over the telephone his voice sounded smooth and attractive. 'I thought you might like to have a bite to eat at a little place I know near to the television studios. It might amuse you to see how the other half lives.'

She laughed. 'I really shouldn't. I've only just come home from a very indulgent weekend, and I ought to be on a diet.'

'Diet? You must be joking with a figure like yours! Oh, come on, Lee, say yes. I'll pick you up around eight. What do you say?'

'Oh well—all right, I'd like to. See you at eight, Keith.'

When she came back into the living room Bridget, who had been unashamedly eavesdropping, grinned at her.

'Well, well! And who's Keith Sands when he's at home?'

Leane told her, enjoying the expression on her face.

'A playwright? Wow! You do seem to have dropped into an interesting life! If I were you I'd be bubbling over with excitement. What was he doing at a party down in darkest Hampshire?'

'He's a friend of Miss Hart, the woman I'm to work for.' Leane sighed. Now she'd let the name slip out. She just wasn't any good at keeping secrets from people, especially Bridget.

'Oh, was she on the stage?' Bridget asked.

'Connected with it, I believe.'

Bridget looked at her thoughtfully. 'You haven't said a lot about her. What's she really like?'

Leane shook her head. 'It's hard to tell after such short acquaintance, but she seems very nice.'

'And what's the operation she's having in Switzerland?'

'Nothing serious—actually it's quite trivial,' Leane said guardedly.

Bridget narrowed her eyes. 'You're very cagey—come on, Lee, I smell a mystery. Let me in on it.'

Leane began to clear away the tea things. 'Heavens! Look at the time! If I'm going to be ready when Keith calls——'

But Bridget took the pile of dishes firmly out of her hands and put them down on the table. 'Oh, no you don't! Here you are going off to Switzerland on some glamorous mission while I stay here emptying bedpans. The very least you can do is to tell about it. If you don't, I'll never speak to you again as long as I live!'

Leane sighed. 'But I promised, Bridget. It would be awful if it got out.'

The other girl shook her head. 'Have I ever let you down, Lee? Haven't we always shared our secrets?'

'Yes, *ours*. This one is someone else's.'

Bridget looked at her for a long moment, her eyes large and pleading, till at last Leane relaxed.

'Oh, all right, I don't suppose it'll matter if you know. But you'll have to promise not to tell a soul.' Bridget silently drew one finger across her throat and Leane went on: 'The woman I'm going to work for is a retired actress who's about to make a comeback. She's going to Switzerland to have facial cosmetic surgery.'

Bridget's mouth dropped open. 'I *see*—all incognito and hush-hush.' She pulled a face. 'Won't you find it rather boring? I mean she won't be ill. There'll be very little nursing for you to do.'

Leane smiled. 'Would you be bored in Switzerland?'

A cushion hit her on the side of the head. 'Trust you!' Bridget said bitterly.

Keith was right on time. As Leane let him into the flat he gasped exaggeratedly. 'Phew! Those stairs! And you talk about dieting. There's enough exercise in those to last me a week!'

Leane introduced Bridget who was pouring the sherry she'd just slipped down to the off-licence to buy. She smiled at him bewitchingly, holding out a glass.

'Drink?'

He took it with a smile. 'Is it a sign of something when one notices the nurses getting prettier and prettier? I must remember to be ill more often.' He raised his glass. 'Cheers!'

But Leane was looking at him oddly. 'How did you know that we were nurses?' she asked.

The smile left his face. 'Ah—well, I just sort of assumed you were—with the hospital just down the road.' He bit his lip and grinned sheepishly. 'Oh dear, I'm going to have to confess, aren't I? I've been asking questions about you, Lee.'

She picked up her coat, unwilling to continue the conversation in front of Bridget who was grinning like a Cheshire cat. 'Goodnight, Bridget,' she said. 'I don't suppose I'll be late.'

Keith winked. 'But don't wait up,' he grinned.

When they were seated in his car he turned to her.

'I get the impression that I've displeased you. Actually it was Adam who told me you were a nurse. Does it matter to you so much—me knowing?'

She relaxed. If Adam had told him it must be all right. She smiled. 'Of course it doesn't matter. I was surprised that you should be so curious about me, that's all.'

He reached out and touched her hand. 'You underestimate yourself, Lee. Ever since last night I've found myself thinking of you almost constantly—wanting to know everything there is to know about you. That's why I'm here now. I reckoned that if you were off to Switzerland in a couple of weeks, I'd better work fast.'

She smiled wryly at him. 'I've an idea you always do!'

He gave her a look of mock reproach. 'Oh, Lee—is that kind?'

She burst out laughing. 'Oh, Keith, you should

make a fortune at writing fiction!'

'I do,' he said, starting the engine, 'and I hope to continue doing so. But I *can* tell the truth—when pressed.'

The restaurant was called The Bay Tree and inside it was cosy and intimate. The walls were covered with signed photographs of every stage and television personality that Leane had ever heard of and more that she hadn't. And, although it was a Monday evening, the place was crowded. The food and wine were excellent, and as they sat over coffee Keith smiled at her across the table.

'I like a girl who isn't afraid to show she's enjoying herself,' he said.

Leane blushed. She felt she might have been talking too much and staring at the celebrities who kept arriving. 'Oh dear,' she said. 'You make me sound like a schoolgirl.'

He laughed. 'I meant it as a compliment. So many of the girls I meet are blasé. They look bored all the time. It seems to be a social necessity, but it does nothing at all for a bloke's ego.' He reached out and covered her hand with his. 'I'd give quite a lot to be in Adam's place.'

She looked up, startled. 'What do you mean?'

He raised an eyebrow. 'Three months in romantic Switzerland with you all to himself! I can't think of anything nicer.'

She shrugged. 'Adam's going to study and besides, he doesn't even like me. We shall spend most of the time keeping out of each other's way, I expect.'

'Huh! He must be mad!' He lit a cigarette and studied her thoughtfully through the smoke. 'He's going to study, eh? Lee—what's the real reason for Romaine's trip?'

She felt her colour rise. 'Why don't you ask *her*?'

'I have—she said she wanted to recharge her batteries before the big comeback.'

'Then you have your answer, so why ask me?'

He pursed his lips. 'I can't help thinking there's more to it. I've known Romaine for a very long time. My father was Godfrey Sands, the actor. He and Romaine worked together a lot in the old days. She never does anything without a good sound reason, sometimes *more* than one!'

Leane shrugged. 'Well I'd say the one she gave you was sound enough. Making a comeback takes strength and courage. I know she wants peace and quiet to study plays too.'

He looked her straight in the eyes. 'And where do you fit into all this, Lee? Why does she need a nurse?'

She took a deep breath. 'When Adam told you I was a nurse, didn't he make it clear that *was* was the operative word? I decided to give it up some time ago. This is a temporary job I've taken while I'm re-thinking my future.'

He nodded. 'I see. I'm barking up the wrong tree, am I?'

She frowned. 'I don't know what you mean.'

He leaned forward. 'It's fairly well known that Romaine has a dicky heart. If her future backers thought it was more serious than she's let them believe they might be rather dismayed.'

Leane laughed, partly with relief. 'I can assure you that Romaine isn't going to Switzerland for heart surgery,' she said firmly. 'In fact there's nothing more to it than you've been told. Romaine simply hopes to come back rested and rejuvenated.'

He sat back with a sigh. 'That's a load off my mind. I'd hate to think of my play taking off only to crash-dive!'

She was quite shocked at the selfishness of his remark and she looked thoughtfully at him for a long moment. For the first time she wondered if he had asked her out this evening merely to find out what he could about Romaine. 'It wouldn't be very nice for her either, would it?' she remarked pointedly.

He stubbed out his cigarette. 'I'll give you a tip about Romaine,' he said quietly. 'She likes young people; she collects them as some people collect butterflies. Just be careful that you don't become part of her collection—like a certain other person I know. If that happened you soon wouldn't be able to call your soul your own.'

She laughed uneasily. 'I'm afraid you're over-dramatising it. But I promise you I'll bear it in mind.'

He drove her home and came with her up the steps of the building, but at the door she turned to him.

'It's very late, Keith.'

He looked at her, his head on one side. 'You mean I'm not invited up for coffee? How can you be so unkind?'

She smiled. 'Remember how the stairs exhausted you?'

He slid his arms round her waist. 'I can think of a rather nice cure for that. But if you insist I won't push—not this time.' He cupped her chin and kissed her lightly. 'Thank you for coming out with me this evening, Lee. Can I see you again?'

She hesitated. 'I'm not sure. I'll have a lot to do before the twenty-sixth. But if I have——'

He kissed her again. 'I'll ring you. At least you can talk to me, can't you?' He looked at her thoughtfully for a moment. 'Lee—let me give you a warning: Don't ever try to take something that belongs to Romaine. She may tell you she hates squabbles, but believe me, she can kick up more fuss than anyone when she's roused. I've seen it happen.' He kissed the tip of her nose. 'Be good, sweetheart. I'll be seeing you.'

She watched as he ran lightly down the steps and got into the car, waving a hand to her as he drove off. He had given her plenty of food for thought if all he said and hinted at were true. His picture of Romaine was a completely different one to hers. He had done nothing to put her mind at rest about the coming three months—quite the contrary.

CHAPTER FIVE

THE days that followed were a whirl of activity for Leane. One of the problems she had was finding a new flat-mate for Bridget. The other girl could not afford to keep the flat on alone. Fortunately, another nurse from St Ann's who was shortly getting married was happy to take Leane's place while she was away.

On the morning of the twenty-sixth the girls were up earlier than usual. Leane's flight left at nine a.m. and she had to be at the airport by eight. Bridget looked a little wistful when she came down to see her friend into the taxi.

'Oh dear, I'm going to miss you quite a lot,' she said. 'You won't forget to write, will you?'

Leane hugged her. 'Of course I won't. Look after yourself, and don't neglect your studying.'

Bridget pulled a face. 'You make it sound dreadfully dull. I wish I were coming with you instead!'

In the taxi, Leane leaned back in her seat. It seemed almost the first moment she had had to relax in the last three weeks. Adam had telephoned her a week ago to tell her the time and number of the flight and she had received her ticket through the post. She was to meet Romaine in the departure lounge. Butterflies fluttered in her stomach as she watched the London streets slide past. She could hardly believe that the day had come at last.

She had not seen Keith again since the night he had taken her out, although he had telephoned her several times. She was afraid she might unwittingly let out something she shouldn't. He seemed very adept at wheedling information out of people.

At the airport she paid off the taxi, checked in her luggage and went through customs. In the departure lounge she looked about her and soon spotted Romaine sitting by herself in a corner. She wore a fur coat with the collar pulled up round her face, a turban-style hat and dark glasses. It seemed she was taking no chances on being recognised.

Leane went up to her. 'Good morning.'

Romaine smiled with relief. 'Oh, how nice to

see you, dear. I do hate these places. All comings and goings; worse than railway stations, though I'll admit, slightly more comfortable.' She stood up. 'Shall we go and have some coffee? We have plenty of time.'

In the cafeteria she told Leane that she had been staying at the Winchester for the past week.

'Edna and Stan have gone ahead with the car,' she explained. 'I let them go earlier to give them a little holiday, and they'll be getting the place ready for us too, of course.'

'Will Adam be joining us?' Leane asked.

'No, we shan't see him until tomorrow,' Romaine told her. 'He's going over by ferry and motoring through France in that terrible Perdita machine of his.' She shook her head. 'Such a nasty uncomfortable old rattletrap! I can't think why he sets such store by the old thing. I'm always telling——'

She broke off as a voice called triumphantly behind them, '*Hello!* I've caught you then!'

They both turned to see Keith Sands standing near their table. He looked breathless and slightly dishevelled.

Romaine gave a surprised start. 'Keith! What on earth are you doing here?'

He pulled out a chair and sat down gratefully, smiling at them. 'I couldn't let my two favourite girls leave the country without a word of farewell, now could I?' He pulled the corners of his mouth down. 'London will be a positive desert without you.'

Romaine gave an impatient little cough. 'Really, Keith! As I live in Hampshire and you hardly know Leane at all I can only assume that you're being facetious as usual. You shouldn't have troubled to come and see us off. I know you never get up until after ten.' She looked at him closely. 'Anyway, how did you know the time of our flight?'

'Actually I went to Leane's flat,' he said with a glint of mischief. 'Her delightful friend Bridget told me—so here I am!' He looked round. 'Where's the redoubtable Dr Blake? Not hiding behind the potted palms trying to avoid me, I hope.'

Leane's lips twitched. 'He's taking his car over by ferry,' she told him.

He sighed with exaggerated relief. 'Good! It's very inhibiting, being disapproved of all the time.'

Silently, Leane agreed.

They only just had time to finish their coffee when their flight number was announced. They gathered up their hand luggage and prepared to leave, and Keith assumed a dejected look.

'I hate goodbyes,' he said dramatically.

'Then you shouldn't have come, dear, should you?' Romaine asked briskly.

He put his hands on her shoulders and kissed her cheek fondly. 'If you get bored and need cheering up, just give me a call,' he said. 'I'll be over in a jiffy.'

Romaine smiled in spite of herself. 'I have no intention of getting bored. I'm going for a rest and with the best will in the world, darling, you could hardly describe yourself as restful, could you?'

He laughed. 'All the same—what's the betting that you'll miss me?'

She patted his cheek and moved away, leaving Leane to deal with him. He looked at her appealingly.

'Well, how about you, Lee—will *you* miss me?'

She laughed and shrugged her shoulders. 'As Romaine said, we hardly know each other.'

He stepped in front of her, barring her way. 'Well, whose fault is that? At least let me kiss you goodbye—give me something to remember.' He slid his arms round her and kissed her lingeringly. 'I may see you sooner than you think,' he whispered enigmatically as he let her go.

She looked up at him, puzzled. 'How? Why?' But at that moment the flight number was called again and she hurried to join Romaine.

'I'll be watching the take-off,' Keith called after her. 'I'll be thinking of you. Send me a postcard of an Alp if you have time!'

When they were comfortably settled in their seats aboard the aircraft Romaine told her that she had been to see John Wilton the day before.

'He was quite taken with your idea of doing a Restoration comedy,' she said. 'He's sending me some scripts to read.'

'What about Keith's play?' Leane asked.

Romaine pulled a face. 'Disappointing. I've promised him that I'll think about it, but quite frankly it's pretty poor. I've tried to encourage the boy because I was once a very dear friend of his poor father's. But I'm afraid his kind of comedy is not for me.'

The journey was uneventful. Romaine slept on the plane and most of the train journey from Zurich was taken up with lunch. A smiling Stan Baker was waiting on the platform of the little station at Lanquart, and soon they were on their way in Romaine's own comfortable saloon, taking the winding mountain road to Mavos. Leane was enthralled by the scenery, the brilliant colours of mountain, grass and sky, the picturesque chalets and the crystal clearness of the air. She exclaimed as much to Romaine, who agreed with her.

'There's nowhere like it on earth. It's sheer heaven, isn't it? But wait till you see our particular corner.'

It was mid-afternoon when they arrived in Mavos. Nestling in a deep valley, the little town looked like something out of a fairy tale with the spires of its three churches dreaming in the sunlight. All around, the mountains towered majestically, their peaks still white with snow, though on the lower slopes the wild alpine flowers were already in bloom.

Stan did not take the road which went through the town, but took a road which curved steeply upwards round the hillside till it levelled out on to a wooded plateau. There the chalet sat, surrounded by young firs and flowering shrubs. Although modern, it was built in the traditional Swiss style in timber; its red roof sweeping low over green-shuttered windows. Edna ran out to meet them as Stan drew the car to a smooth halt, announcing that the kettle was on for a nice cup of tea.

Leane's room had a breathtaking view. She could hardly tear herself away from it, but she made herself unpack and change into trousers and a shirt, hoping she might have time to explore.

Downstairs, she found Romaine relaxing on

the veranda in a long chair. She looked pale, and from force of habit, Leane lifted her wrist and felt for the pulse. Finding it rather fast, she looked at Romaine.

'When you've had your tea, why don't you take a little nap? You were up very early this morning.'

Romaine looked alarmed. 'Why, do I look ill?'

'No, of course not, but you mustn't overdo it.'

'I'm perfectly all right.' Romaine seemed rather affronted. 'What could be better for me than to sit here, breathing in this wonderful air? Besides, Edna has just told me that Otto telephoned to say he'd be over at about four-thirty. It's almost that now.'

'Are you warm enough? Shall I get you a rug?'

Romaine sat up crossly. 'Oh please don't fuss, Leane!' she said crisply. 'I'm not an invalid and I'm not ninety!'

Leane took a step backwards. 'I'm sorry—I just thought——'

'I know you meant it kindly,' Romaine said, 'but I really can't stand fuss. Sit down, dear, and have your tea.'

Leane sat down, rather taken aback, but before she had time to ponder on Romaine's behaviour Edna announced that Dr Kleber had arrived.

He followed her out on to the veranda, a tall distinguished man in his fifties with thick silvery hair and kindly dark eyes. Romaine stood up and held out both hands to him.

'Otto, darling!'

He took her hands, raising them to his lips and kissing each in turn. 'How wonderful to see you again, Romaine.' He looked over her shoulder at

Leane. 'And this must be the delightful companion you told me of in your letter.'

Romaine turned and held out a hand to Leane. 'Of course. I was almost forgetting. Leane Forrest—Dr Otto Kleber.'

The hand that shook hers was firm and capable, and Leane took instantly to the man whose eyes smiled into hers.

'I hear that you are a qualified nurse,' he said. 'You must come over to the clinic and allow me to show you round. I am sure you would find much there to interest you.'

'I'm sure I would,' Leane agreed. 'Thank you very much, I'd love to come.'

'I was rather hoping that Leane would be allowed to stay with me in the theatre when I have my operation, Otto,' Romaine said. 'You will allow that, won't you?'

He inclined his head, smiling gently. 'But of course, if you wish it.'

She glanced at him sideways, fidgeting nervously with her handkerchief. 'Otto, now that you have seen me—do you agree that I need this operation?'

The doctor laughed. 'Dearest Romaine, you do not change! Always looking for the compliments.' He shook his head. 'To me you are quite delightful.'

Romaine frowned. 'But you must think it necessary or you would not have agreed to do it when I sent you the photograph.'

He sat down beside her and took her hand. 'I will tell you my age, Romaine—in case you have forgotten it. I am fifty-five. Being so, more mature ladies appear delightful to me now. But if you wish to look thirty again, this I can do for you—and will, most happily.'

Romaine gave him her most dazzling smile. 'It would be a pity if, after you'd given me a beautiful new face, I no longer appealed to you, Otto,' she said.

The doctor laughed, his dark eyes twinkling merrily. 'Heaven forbid! Even at my great age I can still appreciate the delights of youth!'

Leane smiled to herself. Dr Kleber was skilled in tact as well as surgery.

'But I am forgetting what I came to tell you,' Dr Kleber went on. 'Tomorrow evening, Romaine, when you have had time to settle in, I want you to come into the clinic ready to have tests on the following day. I shall then talk to you about what we are going to do for you and when it is to take place.'

Romaine nodded submissively. 'Of course, Otto, whatever you say.'

When the doctor left, Leane went out to the car with him. As he was getting into it he looked at her. 'How long have you known Romaine?'

'We only met a few weeks ago,' she replied, 'I can't say I know her at all yet. But I hope to.'

He smiled his attractive, winning smile. 'She is a very lovely person, but vulnerable, almost obsessive about her looks—her lost youth. But the significance of that should not be minimised.'

Leane nodded. 'I understand. That's why you agreed to do the operation for her?'

He sighed. 'The state of the mind is important; so little can tip the balance. Many women are unaffected by the appearance of a few lines— happy to accept the passing of time. Not so,

Romaine.' He smiled again. 'But no matter. I shall make her as lovely and as youthful as when I first knew her.'

As she watched him drive away, Leane thought how lucky Romaine was to have such an understanding doctor, but later, as they sat together after dinner, Romaine grew reminiscent and Dr Kleber's compassion became clearer to her.

'He's still handsome, isn't he?' Romaine asked dreamily. Leane agreed and she went on: 'We were once very much in love, you know. But that was a very long time ago—before you were even born, I daresay. It was when he was a medical student in England, and I was just beginning in the theatre.' She smiled wistfully. 'What fun we had! It was such a happy, carefree time.'

'What happened?' Leane asked gently.

Romaine sighed and lifted her shoulders. 'There were his exams—my work too. I was moving around the country a lot in those days. We were both ambitious. Otto had a fierce determination to be a good doctor—the best. I was equally determined to become a star.'

'So it faded?'

Romaine nodded. 'I'm afraid so, though we always kept in touch. When I had my first leading part in the West End Otto wrote. He always sent me flowers on every first night, and when he was in London he would come to see the show and come round afterwards to take me to supper, just like in the old days.' She sighed. 'But it was never quite the same after we were both successful.'

There was a wistful silence as she gazed into

the fire and Leane prompted: 'Did he ever marry—Dr Kleber?'

'No, neither of us did,' Romaine replied. 'You know, there's nothing quite like that first love. Nothing else ever quite comes up to it. There have been many men in my life but none of them had that special something I was looking for.' She sighed. 'Perhaps it's all a dream really. Perhaps no one *ever* finds it.' She looked at Leane speculatively. 'Is there no one special in your life?'

'There was,' Leane admitted, 'but I know now that it wasn't the real thing. Just a teenage crush that developed into a habit. We both grew out of it.'

Romaine leaned forward to pat her hand. 'Take a tip from me, my dear, when you find the right man hold on to him, hard. Never mind the obstacles that might seem to be in the way. I know now that the saddest thing in life is to miss out on love.'

Leane was awake early next morning, in time to see the sun rising above the mountain tops when she folded back the wooden shutters from her window. The tingling fresh air and the view from the chalet made her long to explore, but again it was not to be; Romaine demanded her attention all morning. Her relaxed mood of the previous evening was gone and she was jumpy and irritable. Unpacking, she had found her clothes to be crumpled and she insisted on everything being pressed before she would put it away.

'I should never have let Edna go on ahead,' she said petulantly. 'I'm hopeless at packing. Look at my things! They look like something from a jumble sale!'

Nothing was right. She wanted the furniture in her room moved round. The coffee was too strong—the water not hot enough. Leane knew it was bad for her to get so agitated, but she hesitated to behave too much like a nurse after Romaine's reaction last night.

Finally, it was Edna who calmed her down.

'Now, now, Madam,' she said, sounding for all the world like a patient nanny, 'you really must not get so riled. Miss Forrest and Stan and me will soon have things the way you like them. Just you leave it all to us. Dr Blake'll be here soon and you don't want him to see you all of a tizz, now do you?'

'I am *not* in a tizz!' Romaine said indignantly. But nevertheless, she calmed down.

It was just before lunch that they heard the familiar roar of Perdita's engine negotiating the mountain road. Romaine had invited Leane to have a pre-lunch sherry with her on the veranda, and she stood up excitedly as the car breezed in through the gates.

'Adam, darling!' She ran down the steps to meet him, followed by Leane.

He got out of the car smiling and Romaine grasped both his hands. 'Oh, I'm so relieved to see you here safe and sound. Leane will tell you, I've been edgy all morning, worrying about you in that dreadful car. Tell me, did you have a good journey? Would you like a bath first or are you hungry?'

Adam laughed. 'Give me time and I'll answer all your questions. You look fine anyway.' His eyes moved to where Leane stood. 'Hello, Lee. How do you like Mavos?'

'It's very beautiful—what I've seen so far.' Her voice was cool and steady but she was quite dismayed at the pounding of her own heart—at the disturbance within her as their eyes met.

Over lunch Romaine was thoughtful. 'Otto came to welcome us last night,' she told Adam. 'He tells me I'm to go into the clinic tonight and spend tomorrow having tests.'

Adam nodded. 'That's quite usual.' He glanced at her. 'You're not worrying, are you? Would you like Leane or me to come with you?'

She shook her head. 'No, I'm not in the least worried, not with Otto to look after me. It's just that I'm feeling rather guilty. I've kept poor Leane on the go ever since she's been here. It must have been so frustrating not to be able to go out and look round. So while I'm away tomorrow, why don't you take her out for the day—show her the sights?'

Leane coloured. 'You mustn't mind me. I'm here to work, after all.'

'Nevertheless, I insist,' Romaine said firmly. 'What do you think, Adam? Isn't it a good idea?'

Leane hardly dared to look at him. It was most embarrassing. He could hardly refuse; it was practically an order. 'I—I'm sure there must be a dozen things you'd rather do,' she stammered. 'I can quite easily explore by myself.'

But when she raised her eyes she saw that he was looking straight at her across the table. 'Unless you actually object, Lee, I'd love to show you round.'

Romaine looked from one to the other and laughed. 'Oh, dear! How very formal you are! I hope a day spent in each other's company will make you seem more like friends.'

During the afternoon Dr Kleber telephoned to ask if Romaine would have dinner with him that evening, and at six o'clock he collected her in his car. Leane and Adam waved them off from the veranda. As the car disappeared through the gates Adam turned to her.

'Would you like to eat out this evening? We might go to the Postli. It's one of the oldest buildings in the valley, and used to be a kind of coaching inn. A real bit of old Switzerland. Would you like that?'

Leane smiled. 'It sounds lovely—but there's no need. I mean, you mustn't feel obliged to ask me because of what Romaine said.'

He sighed and the thick brows came together. 'I don't "feel obliged", as you put it. Look, Lee, let's get one thing straight: I'm not a child—or a lapdog either.'

The outside of the Postli was like something from a picture book. Standing in the main street of the village, cheek by jowl with more modern buildings, the old inn was built all of timber and decorated with traditional carving and painted flowers. Inside, the restaurant was warm and cosy with a bar at one end and a small dance floor at the other. The waitresses wore Swiss costume and the tables were covered in chequered cloths. In the centre of each burned a single candle. A small band played traditional Swiss music, interspersed with the occasional pop number. Leane looked round with delight as they seated themselves at a corner table.

'Oh, it's lovely! The thing I love about Switzerland is that everything is just as I'd expected it to be. Not only as good, but better!'

Adam smiled. 'I think I can safely say that the same can be said of the food.' He passed her the menu. 'What will you try?'

The meal was delicious, and when they had eaten Adam asked her if she would like to dance. As they circled the tiny floor she asked him about Romaine's tests. 'Is there any possibility that her heart condition will prevent her from having the operation?'

He shook his head. 'It's only slight. She was advised that with rest, the right diet and exercise the condition could clear up. That was when she bought Heathridge House and moved to the New Forest.'

'So you don't think she's in any danger?'

He frowned. 'Let's put it this way—I feel that the stress caused by not having the operation would do more harm than the op. itself.'

She looked up at him. 'Dr Kleber said more or less the same thing to me last night. And of course she'll be having a local anaesthetic.'

'That's right. Most cosmetic surgery is done under a local these days.' He looked down at her. 'I think that's enough shop for tonight, don't you? Now—about this day out we're to have tomorrow; where would you like to go?'

After some discussion they decided on a day exploring the village, maybe making a trip up the Schatzalp in the cable car in the afternoon. 'We could ask Edna to make up a picnic lunch,' Adam said. 'We could take one of the mountain walks and eat it by a waterfall.'

'That sounds wonderful!' Leane's eyes sparkled as she smiled at him. Across the table his hand covered hers briefly.

'I'm glad you came, Lee,' he said quietly. 'And I'm sorry about the bad start we made. I think we understand each other now though.'

Leane felt the breath catch in her throat at the touch of his hand. 'I hope so, Adam,' she said.

When they came out of the hotel the moon had risen. The sky was like diamond-studded black velvet and the huge snow-clad mountains seemed to cluster protectively round the village, which was now ablaze with lights. Leane felt her heart lift as she turned to Adam.

'I know what Romaine means when she says this is the most beautiful place on earth,' she said. 'Do you know, I saw the sun rise this morning. It turned the snow on the mountain tops to pure gold. I saw it from my window. I never saw anything so beautiful in my whole life.'

He stood looking down at her for a long moment. 'Neither did I,' he said quietly. Then he took her face gently between his hands and kissed her softly on the mouth.

CHAPTER SIX

BEFORE she got into bed that night, Leane folded back the shutters and opened the bedroom window. The air was clean and so cold that it took her breath away. She looked out at the silver-blue of the mountain tops, the stars twinkling overhead and the village below her, glittering like a jewelled toy: one would have to be made of wood not to feel romantic on such a night, she told herself.

The truth was that she had been profoundly stirred by Adam's kiss. Why couldn't she laugh it off as she did when Keith kissed her? She knew the answer to that deep inside, but she would not acknowledge it, even to herself. Adam's first consideration, she knew, was his work. His second was Romaine. He was here for the benefit of both, and he was being pleasant to her for Romaine's sake. As long as she remembered to keep that in mind she would be safe. But, lying in bed with the moon shining in at the open window, it was very hard to keep the romantic images from flitting through her sleepy mind.

When she came downstairs the following morning she found Adam waiting. He had already asked Edna to pack them a picnic lunch, and as they ate their hot rolls and drank their coffee she stole a glance at him. It was odd how different he seemed—she could hardly believe he was the same man who had interviewed her a month ago—the man she had thought so pompous. Could it be the casual clothes he wore, or was he more relaxed here in Switzerland?

He caught her looking at him and smiled.

'You look nice, but don't forget to take something warm to wear,' he said. 'It can be very cold at the top of the mountains, even on a sunny day like this. People tend to forget the altitude.'

In daytime the village was as busy and bustling as an English market town, and Leane found the shops full of exciting things, especially the beautiful hand embroidery and knitwear. They had coffee at a pavement café, surrounded by tubs of colourful flowers, and when they had rested they set out on their mountain walk, crossing the streets that ran one above the other like a series of terraces, linked by cobbled alleys, under which the spring water babbled happily on its way to the lake.

Eventually the streets petered out and they took a steep, stony path that wound upwards. Leane's feet began to drag and Adam turned, holding out his hand to her.

'Not much farther, then we can rest,' he said. 'There's a little church just ahead with a sort of plateau in front. There's a seat there with a wonderful view.'

He was right. The stretch of ground in front of the little white church had a seat, placed at a point where one could look down on to the valley. Leane sank on to it gratefully.

'I'd no idea we'd come so far. No wonder I'm so exhausted.'

Adam sat beside her. 'You should do this walk every morning before breakfast, as I always do when I'm here. It's marvellous for getting you in trim, and there's nothing like this air.' He took a deep breath, letting it out with a sigh of appreciation.

Leane looked at him. 'How many times have you been here before?' she asked.

'Only twice. Once as a student when a bunch of us came on a winter sports holiday, and once with Romaine, about eighteen months ago when she came to see Dr Kleber.'

She nodded. 'You've known her a long time, haven't you?'

'Most of my life really,' he told her. 'She was

friendly with the people who brought me up. It was in the Midlands, and she used to stay with them sometimes when she was touring in her early years in the theatre. I can't really remember a time when I didn't know her. Since my foster parents died I've seen even more of her, especially since her illness.'

The bell in the little church tower began to toll with a rich, mellow sound that echoed round the valley and the sound of childish voices floated upwards as a crocodile of little girls from the convent wound its way up the path led by two smiling nuns. Leane took a deep breath and leaned back.

'Oh, I'm *so* glad I came! I wouldn't have missed this for the world!'

Adam turned his head to look at her. Her cheeks glowed with colour and her eyes were shining with the delight of it all.

'Lee,' he said hesitantly. 'I'd like to explain about the bad start we made. It was my fault. I don't know if I can make you understand, but when I saw you throwing away your career it was like a reflection of my own actions.'

She looked at him in surprise. 'But you're not ending your career, you're furthering it!'

He sighed. 'On the face of it, yes. But when Romaine made me the offer and I accepted, I wasn't sure that I was doing it for the right reasons. I'd only just convinced myself that I was when you came along and made me uncertain all over again.'

Leane looked around her. 'I admit that all this must have been very tempting, but surely you must have known, if you were truthful with yourself?'

He looked away. 'That's something I'm not always very good at, facing the truth. When I interviewed you and you were so honest about opting out——'

'I didn't exactly opt out, Adam,' she said quickly. 'Something happened to make me reassess my situation.'

He looked into her eyes. 'At a guess I'd say it was something of an emotional nature. The patient who died—were you in love with him? Was that it?'

She stared at him. 'Good heavens, no!' She told him about that night in Casualty—about the man who had gone into cardiac arrest when she had taken him to be drunk. When she had finished he shook his head.

'It's the same story in so many hospitals—shortage of staff, not negligence. By leaving you only made that situation worse. Good nurses are like gold.'

She sighed. 'That's just it, I'm not so sure that I *am* a good nurse. That was why I gave it up. I felt that at least I must have a break—a breathing space. Time to get things into perspective.'

He smiled, his serious expression melting. 'Well I won't argue with the sense of that. And you certainly couldn't have found a better place to take it.' He stood up and held out his hand. 'Shall we move on?'

They walked on up the mountain path which twisted and wound its way through the trees. At one point Leane heard something skittering behind her through the pine-needles and turned to see a fat red squirrel scrabbling away at a tree-root just a few feet away, quite unconcerned at her presence. Fascinated, she touched Adam's arm and pointed. He laughed.

'They're as tame as pet kittens,' he said. 'You watch.' He sat down on the dry pine needles and reached into the picnic basket for an apple. Almost immediately the squirrel ran across and sat up confidently in front of him, waiting bright-eyed for a titbit. As though by magic three more joined him, and one of them even climbed on to Adam's shoulder. Leane laughed with delight.

'I wish I'd known about them. I'd have brought some nuts.'

Adam stood up, scattering the last fragments of the apple. 'I'd quite forgotten about them, or I would have told you.'

On they climbed, pausing from time to time to look down through the trees into the valley. They walked over a wooden bridge that crossed the funicular track and watched as one rumbled on the upward journey.

'We'll try that another day,' Adam promised.

One more steep slope and they reached the place Adam had been heading for. A clearing in the trees revealed a sheer cliff face, over which cascaded a ribbon of sparkling water. Leane stood enraptured.

'Oh—how lovely!' She turned to him and laughed. 'I never seem to stop saying that, do I? It must be getting monotonous.'

He smiled and shook his head. 'Seeing you look like that could never be monotonous. You know, there was a time when I thought you *couldn't* smile.'

Leane smiled wryly. 'I seem to remember a

crack about my stiff upper lip,' she said.

He put down the basket and put his hands on her shoulders, turning her to face him. 'Will you believe me when I tell you that it was that very stubborn look of yours that made me behave so badly that night at Romaine's dinner party?' he said. 'I suddenly wanted to know what it would be like to see that mouth soften—to feel it relax under mine.' He looked into her eyes. 'And when it smiles I find it even more irresistible.'

When his lips met hers this time it was more than a brief kiss. His lips clung searchingly to hers, making her head spin dizzily. She closed her eyes and after a moment her arms slipped round him. As they drew apart he looked down at her, his eyes searching hers.

'You once said that you liked things that "made people come alive",' he said. 'Do you remember?'

She nodded breathlessly. 'I—I was talking about your car.'

'I'm not talking about the car now, Lee,' he said. 'I'm talking about you. I've never seen you look more alive than you do at this moment. Will you tell me why? Is it the mountains? Is it being in Switzerland? Or could it be something else?'

She laughed shakily and pushed him gently away. 'It wouldn't do to analyse a thing like that, would it?' she said lightly. 'It would be like trying to analyse a sunset. It would destroy the magic.' She turned to the picnic basket. 'Shall we eat over there in that patch of sunlight near the water?'

The moment was gone and she was relieved.

From the moment that Adam had kissed her she had known without a doubt that nothing would ever be quite the same again. She would never have dreamed that the touch of his lips would have such a shattering effect on her.

She was trembling as she spread out the appetising food that Edna had packed, but she chattered animatedly to hide her true feelings. As she handed Adam a plate she glanced at him.

'You apologised for the bad start we made, and you said it was all your fault. That isn't quite true. I did my share. The things I said in the car that day on the way back to London—the night before too—I—implied things about you and Romaine.' She glanced at him expectantly, hoping he would realise that she was offering him a chance to explain what he was doing in Romaine's room that night. Surely there must be a simple explanation? But Adam just smiled.

'That's all over and done with now,' he said, reaching for her hand. 'We'll pretend we've only just met for the first time, shall we?'

And there was nothing she could do but agree.

When they had finished eating they tidied their litter into the basket and made their way down the mountain path again. The cable car that ran up the Schatzalp was on the other side of the village. They bought their tickets and crowded into the car when it rumbled to a halt at the little platform. The wooden seats that ran around the inside were soon taken, and the other passengers stood, filling the space in the middle. Adam and Leane managed to stand at the end, near the window. In the crush Leane felt his fingers curl firmly round hers. She looked up at him a little apprehensively.

'Is it safe? They seem to allow an awful lot of people on.'

He squeezed her hand. 'It's always like this. You're not nervous, are you?'

'No.' She smiled. 'I've been thinking about Romaine, though.'

The relaxed look left his face. 'She'll be fine, don't worry.'

But Leane couldn't help worrying—and not wholly about Romaine's operation, which made her feel guilty.

The cable car went up in two stages, and it was necessary to change cars halfway. When they got out they saw that there was a restaurant with a magnificent glazed-in balcony built out over the edge of the mountainside. Adam suggested that they have tea there on the way down.

'Switzerland seems to be the only Continental country where they can make tea almost like the English,' he said.

When they got out at the summit Leane shivered and pulled on the thick woolly she'd brought with her. The sun shone brilliantly, but the air was so cold that it almost took her breath away.

'It hits the back of your throat like an iced drink,' she laughed, gasping a little.

Adam put an arm round her. 'Let's walk,' he said.

The view was incredible, like something from another planet; nothing but mountain tops as far as the eye could see. A group of young men passed them, carrying hang-gliding equipment.

'That must be a wonderful feeling,' Leane

remarked. 'To glide freely with the wind—like being a bird. At one with the elements.'

Adam smiled down at her. 'Funny, but I don't need to hang-glide to feel like that today,' he told her.

By the time they got back into the cable car for the return descent the weather had changed dramatically. A thick mist swirled around them, damp and chill. Leane shivered.

'It seems we came just in time. There'll be nothing more to see this afternoon by the look of it.'

Adam pulled her close to his side, an arm round her shoulders. 'I must say I'm looking forward to that tea when we get to the halfway stage,' he said.

They found to their surprise that they were the only two passengers in the car on the return journey, and when they went into the restuarant that was empty too. They took a table on the balcony and Leane shrugged out of her woolly jacket.

'It's nice to feel warm again.' She peered out through the window. Down here the mist had turned to rain, the mountain tops were obscured by cloud and the valley below was hazy. When the waitress brought their tea she asked why there were no other customers.

The girl smiled shyly and tried to explain in halting English: 'Soon there comes the storm— with the thunder and the lightning. The cable car must not go then. All the people go down before this can happen.'

Leane looked at Adam in alarm. 'Oh, dear! Perhaps we should go now. We'll be marooned!'

But the words were hardly out of her mouth

when a blinding flash of lightning split the sky, followed by a crash of thunder. Leane jumped violently, but the waitress smiled placidly.

'Please do not worry. You are quite safe here. The storm makes much noise but is usually over soon. Make yourselves comfortable. You would perhaps like something to eat?'

Adam nodded. 'A good idea. Some of those delicious pastries, I think.' When the girl had gone he reached for Leane's hand. 'You're not really afraid of the storm, are you?'

She laughed shakily. 'Well—let's just say that I'm glad you're here.'

He squeezed her fingers. 'We're really lucky to have this grandstand view of it. Mountain storms can be quite impressive.' He drew his chair closer to hers and put an arm round her. 'Is that better?'

They watched as one clap of thunder followed another, the lightning cutting across the dark sky with momentary flashes of steel-like brilliance, chillingly splendid. The roar of the thunder bounced off the surrounding mountains, one clap close on the echo of the last, till the whole valley was like a vast bubbling cauldron. Leane gave an involuntary shudder.

'Cold?' Adam asked.

She shook her head. 'Just awed. It makes one feel very small and insignificant somehow.'

He touched her cheek, cradling it with his hand, turning her face towards his till their eyes met. His lips brushed hers and she caught her breath.

'Not—not here,' she whispered, but he was gathering her close.

'There's no one here but us,' he said, his lips

moving against hers. 'Something has happened to me today, Lee. I'm bewitched. I want to go on kissing you for ever.' His arms tightened round her, but suddenly she was remembering something that Keith had said.

'Don't ever try to take something that belongs to Romaine.'

He hadn't been talking of material possessions. He had meant people—Romaine's 'collection' of people, in which Adam held a major position. If she gave in to her emotions she could be playing with fire. She pushed him gently but firmly away.

'I believe the storm is dying,' she said, staring straight in front of her at the cooling tea on the table.

He didn't speak—didn't take his eyes from her face.

'What is it, Lee?' he asked at last. 'Have I said something to offend you?'

She bit her lip. 'No, of course not.' She longed to throw herself into his arms, to hold him close and respond to his kisses with all the feeling that welled up within her, but how could she? He obviously meant so much to Romaine. If she allowed herself to fall in love with Adam she could not remain under Romaine's roof, pretending to be indifferent. Could *he*? Was this merely a game to him?

'Leane,' he said, touching her lips with his fingertips, 'don't go away from me now. I've never felt like this before. Oh, there have been girls, but not—not like this. I felt it was the same for you. Do you——'

She stood up, panic rising inside her. 'I—I

don't know. Please, Adam, I think we should go now.' She hurried from the restaurant and out into the rain; ran across to the cable car station and stood shivering on the boarded platform, her damp shirt clinging to her shoulders. A moment later he joined her and silently wrapped the woollen jacket round her shaking shoulders.

'You forgot it,' he said. 'You'll catch cold.' Then: 'I won't rush you, Lee. Please don't look so unhappy. Is there—someone else—at home? Is that it?'

'No!' She spun round to look at him. 'Not for *me*, anyway.'

He looked into her eyes trying to read what he saw there. 'Or for me—so what is it, darling? Why——?'

They heard the wires sing as the cable car started up again, then a whine and rumble as it began to descend. He drew her gently to him and kissed her, his eyes dark and intent as he looked into hers. 'You *do* feel the same, Lee. Don't say you don't, please.'

She closed her eyes, afraid that he would read what was in them and she was grateful for the cable car's arrival so that she didn't have to answer his urgent question.

Inside sat the bedraggled members of the hang-gliding team who had been stranded at the summit during the storm. They looked thwarted and uncommunicative. Adam nudged her and whispered:

'What price being "at one with the elements" now?'

No other conversation was possible, but he

held her hand in a firm, warm grip all the way to the bottom.

There was just time to bath and change before Edna tapped on the door to tell her of Romaine's return.

'Madam's just got home, dear,' she said, putting her head round the door. 'The doctor's with her, and they'd like to see you.'

Leane hurried downstairs to find Romaine looking flushed and excited in the drawing room. She sat on the settee, a glass of sherry in her hand, while Adam spoke to Dr Kleber over by the window. When she saw Leane, Romaine held out her hands.

'Oh there you are, dear. I hope you're none the worse for your soaking. What do you think? I'm to go into the clinic tomorrow evening and have my operation the following day! Isn't it exciting?' She took both Leane's hands in hers, her eyes shining.

'That's wonderful news,' Leane said.

'You will stay with me all the time, won't you dear?' she asked anxiously. 'I shan't mind any of it if you're there. Otto says Adam may stand in too, as he will on all the operations at the clinic from now on.'

They were joined by the two men and Romaine addressed herself to Adam. 'Did you show Leane the lake today? I thought perhaps we might all go there tomorrow, perhaps take our lunch?'

'I want you to rest tomorrow, Romaine,' Otto Kleber told her. 'And I want these two young people to come over to the clinic for a tour of the place. It will be as well if they are familiar with it.' He smiled. 'I promise to let you have them back by lunchtime, though.'

Romaine flapped her hands at him. 'You're a terrible bully, Otto. But I have no choice but to give in, I suppose.' She began to talk to Adam and Dr Kleber took Leane by the arm and moved away a little.

'I think that the sooner I operate the better,' he said quietly. 'She is more nervous than she will admit. Have you seen cosmetic surgery before?'

'No. What do you propose to do?' Leane asked.

'I shall remove the surplus tissue from around the eyes and tighten the jawline,' he told her. 'It's a relatively simple piece of surgery. The incisions will be made close to the lower lashes and behind the ears so that the scars will be almost invisible even from the beginning.'

'Will there be a lot of bruising?'

He pursed his lips. 'After the first day bruising does appear, though I pride myself on keeping it to the minimum. Romaine may wish to wear dark glasses for a week to ten days, and I shall insist that she rests even though she should not feel any ill effects. With that heart condition we must take no chances with shock.'

Leane nodded. 'Don't worry, Doctor, I'll take good care of her. It will give her the chance she needs to read the manuscripts she brought with her.'

He smiled. 'She is fond of you. It is good that she has the company of two people of whom she is fond. There are no relatives at all, I believe?'

'None that I've heard of.'

He nodded. 'I too have none. It is a sad state of affairs. One needs loving sympathy at such times.' He held up his hand and called across the room to Romaine: 'I must go now. I will see you tomorrow.'

She turned to him in dismay. 'Oh, Otto, can't you stay to dinner?'

He wagged a finger at her. 'You must not tempt me. Already I am neglecting my work because of you, you wicked woman. I promise you that the day after tomorrow you shall have my undivided attention. And this evening you must look for a gift which I shall send you.' He kissed her fingertips and was gone.

When his gift arrived just after dinner it was a rose bush planted in a pot. Romaine read the card which was attached and passed it to Leane, her eyes misty. It read:

'My dearest Romaine, I remember that your favourite flower is the Iceberg rose. As you know, rose-growing is my relaxation, and I have grown this one especially for you. Put it on your balcony and watch it bloom as you bloom yourself. Yours ever—Otto.'

Leane looked up. 'What a sweet gesture. And he remembered your favourite flower after all these years.' She fingered the delicate buds on the little bush. 'You'll be able to watch the buds open as you lie in bed after the operation. That's what he intends, isn't it?'

Later that night on her way to bed she met Adam in the corridor. 'Goodnight, Adam,' she whispered. 'I forgot to thank you for a lovely day. I enjoyed it very much.'

'Did you?' He looked at her. 'Was it *really* a lovely day for you?'

She couldn't meet his eyes, dark and direct, and she made to move on, but he caught her arm.

'I wish I could believe you, Lee. I wish I could see inside your mind and find out what you really feel.' He touched her cheek but she stood quite still, her arms at her sides, willing herself not to surrender to the longing that overwhelmed her.

Half an hour later she passed Romaine's door on her way to the bathroom and paused. Should she go in and see if she was sleep? Perhaps she would appreciate someone to talk to. But as she softly turned the handle a sound made her stop. Romaine was not alone. She was talking to someone—and the voice that mingled with hers was Adam's.

CHAPTER SEVEN

The reception hall of the Kleber Clinic had more the atmosphere of a luxury hotel than a hospital. Deep pile carpet in a restful shade of olive green covered the floor, and there were flowers and plants everywhere. Adam and Leane waited in comfortable chairs whilst the beautifully groomed girl at the reception desk telephoned up to Otto's office to tell him of their arrival.

Leane looked across at Adam and her heart gave a painful lurch. She could hardly bear to think of yesterday. It seemed now as though none of it had actually happened—like something she had dreamed. How could he have seriously meant the things he had said to her, only to join Romaine in her room late last night? It was true that he owed a lot to her generosity, but need he show his gratitude quite so ardently? The thought sickened her, and she resolved that from now on she would put all thoughts of a close relationship with Adam right out of her mind.

'You're very quiet this morning, Lee.'

She gave a start as he leaned towards her and she felt the hot colour stain her cheeks, but at that moment the doors of the lift opened and Dr Kleber stepped out, accompanied by a tall elegant blonde girl in a white coat.

'Ah, good morning my friends,' he smiled. 'Allow me to present my assistant, Dr Helga Stein—Dr Adam Blake—Miss Leane Forrest.' As the three exchanged polite greetings he went onn: 'As I shall be in surgery all day tomorrow I have much to do today, so Dr Stein will show you round. Will you come to my office afterwards for coffee?'

The blonde girl smiled, showing perfect white teeth.

'Please, will you come this way.'

They went up in the lift to the first floor and were shown the room that Romaine would occupy. It had a wonderful view of the lake from its wide balcony, and there was an adjoining bathroom, telephone, T.V. and radio.

'All the rooms are the same as this,' Dr Stein told them, 'except that they are decorated in different colours. Perhaps you would like to see the day rooms? They are on the other side of the building.'

There were two day rooms. Both were large, airy and comfortable, but one was furnished for relaxation whilst the other had two walls lined with books and was furnished with writing-tables equipped with stationery. Both rooms had sliding glass doors leading to an attractive terraced garden that looked on to the mountains.

'Many of our patients are businessmen, and like to have somewhere to work while they are recovering,' Helga Stein explained. 'We also have a great many accident cases referred to us,' she went on, 'and burns. Dr Kleber is famous for his brilliant skin grafts, as I expect you know.' She gave Adam her dazzling smile. 'But I understand that you are to be studying with us for the summer, Dr Blake. I'm sure you will find much to interest you here.'

Adam returned her smile. 'I'm sure I shall—and please, call me Adam.'

Leane's heart sank. She felt plain and insignificant beside this tall, elegant girl with her golden skin and pale gleaming hair. She and Adam had so much in common—they were to work together closely too—she shut the thought firmly out of her mind, telling herself that it could make no possible difference to her.

They got back into the lift again and went up to the top floor where the operating theatre was situated. Leane was fascinated. She had never seen such up-to-date equipment, and for a while her own worries were forgotten as she looked round and listened to Helga Stein's commentary. As arranged, they all met in Dr Kleber's office for coffee when the tour of inspection was over and later, as they settled themselves into the car, Leane was surprised to find that it was already twelve o'clock.

'This morning has flown!' she remarked. 'What did you think of the clinic?'

'Magnificent.' Adam sighed. 'If only one could

bring Dr Kleber's methods within the reach of people who can't afford them.'

She looked at him. 'Well, thanks to Romaine you may soon be able to do just that. I'm sure it's what you both wish, isn't it?'

He nodded thoughtfully, then asked, out of the blue, 'Do you drive, Lee?'

She looked up in surprise. 'Yes—though I haven't had much practise since I passed the test.'

'Then it's time you did. Would you like to try now?'

She stared at him. 'You mean in your car—in Perdita?'

'Of course. Why not?' He began to get out. 'Come on, no time like the present.'

Flustered, Leane began to make excuses. 'But I *can't!* I've never driven on the wrong side before!'

He laughed. 'In my experience most women do that anyway! You should feel perfectly at home!'

Although she had her heart in her mouth, she took the wheel and managed to get back to the chalet without incident, flushing with pleasure when Adam congratulated her.

'I knew you could do it. Now you can take Perdita whenever you need her.'

But Leane wasn't so sure. It seemed to her that Adam had offered to let her drive merely to steer the conversation away from Romaine.

Over lunch Adam chatted brightly about their tour of the clinic, making special reference to Helga Stein.

'She seems most efficient and she's certainly a

very attractive woman. I'm sure you'll like her, Romaine.'

Romaine looked up from her plate and pursed her lips.

'I met her yesterday, and I'm not sure that I like her type—all cold efficiency and icy calm. It seems to me that women doctors have far less sympathy than male ones.'

Adam laughed. 'That's rather a sweeping statement. I'm sure that Dr Stein is very kind and sympathetic. She was telling us about the accident and burns cases they treat. I'm looking forward to seeing some of those.'

Romaine laid down her knife and fork. 'She was at great pains to tell me about them too; all those *worthier* cases. I got the distinct impression that she considered me a selfish, vain old woman with more money than sense.' She looked across the table at Leane, her eyes suddenly brimming with tears. 'Perhaps it's true. Do I really appear like that?'

Instantly Adam was at her side, taking both of her hands in his and looking earnestly into her eyes. 'Of course it isn't true, Romaine,' he said. 'You're just feeling a bit nervy and down this morning, that's all. I'm quite sure Dr Stein wasn't getting at you. I expect she thought you'd be interested—that it might take your mind off your own operation to hear about others. Why should she criticise you?'

Romaine looked at him, her lip trembling. 'You're right, why should she? I'm paying enough, after all.' She fumbled for a handkerchief. 'Sometimes I think I wouldn't have any friends at all if it weren't for my money.'

Adam took her by the shoulders and shook her gently. 'Now, you're not to talk like that. Do you hear?' He glanced at Leane, who came round the table to them.

'Please don't upset yourself, Romaine,' she said quietly. 'Dr Kleber said you were to rest. You must be calm and relaxed for tomorrow. I think you know that what you're saying is nonsense. Dr Kleber is your devoted friend and you have Adam—me, too, if you can look on me as your friend as well as an employee.'

Romaine looked at each of them, sniffing back the threatening tears. 'You're both right, of course. I'm making a complete fool of myself. Please finish your lunch and forget what I said.'

Leane laid a hand on her arm. 'This afternoon you must let Adam take you out alone. I had a whole day off yesterday, and besides, I should really spend the afternoon packing the things you'll need for your stay in hospital.'

Romaine smiled, obviously pleased at the thought of having Adam to herself for the afternoon. 'Oh, Leane, dear. Are you sure you wouldn't like to come too? Edna can easily pack for me.'

Leane shook her head. 'I think perhaps I'm more familiar with what you'll need for two nights in hospital. You go off and have a relaxed afternoon and come back calm and refreshed.'

She watched from Romaine's window as they drove off after lunch, heading for the lake with a picnic basket in the back of the car. As Adam nosed Perdita skilfully down the winding track to the road below and they vanished from sight among the trees, she turned from the window with a sigh, then started a little as she saw Edna, who had just come in.

'I thought maybe you could do with some help, dear,' the older woman said kindly. 'Then when we've finished perhaps you'd like to have tea in the garden with Stan and me. No need to be on your own.'

It didn't take long to pack Romaine's small case and tidy the room, and Leane was glad of Edna's offer of company for tea. Stan had it all ready in the garden when they went down, and the three of them settled down happily on the leaf-dappled lawn. She learned that Stan and Edna had been with Romaine ever since she had retired from the stage, and that they were both devoted to her.

'No one could be a better employer,' Stan said, sitting back and lighting his pipe. 'When our married daughter, Mary, was taken ill with appendicitis last year, she insisted on paying for her to have a holiday afterwards with the kids.'

Edna nodded agreement. 'She sent me straight off to look after things while Mary was in hospital too,' she said. 'Kindness itself, she is, when you have any trouble. Of course, she has her moods—her ups and downs, but then, don't we all?'

'I'm afraid she was a little down this morning,' Leane said. 'She's got it into her head that people think her selfish and vain, spending so much on her appearance.'

Edna clicked her tongue. 'Poor Madam. I can understand her. She's got nothing but her looks and her career when it comes down to it, has she? Money's no substitute for a family. As for selfish—you should see the cheques she sends to different charities, especially the children's.'

Stan took his pipe out of his mouth and nodded wisely. 'A real lady, Madam is. And she's real fond of young Dr Blake too. Only lives for his visits. I'm sure I don't know what she'd do without him.'

Leane felt her heart quicken. 'But surely—he'll marry some day, and then——' She looked at Stan and Edna, who exchanged knowing glances.

'That's something we've often said,' Edna replied. 'Anyone Dr Blake marries will have a rare rival in Madam—oh, not that I'm suggesting that there's anything there shouldn't be between them, but still——'

Stan chuckled. 'I reckon the girl'd have to be tough to stand up to the going-over she'd get before she was passed as A.1.' He shook his head. 'But then I reckon that if he were the marrying kind he'd have done it before this.'

Edna began to stack the tea things on to the tray. 'Too dedicated to his profession and to Madam, if you ask me,' she said. 'I mean—I don't see how he ever gets time for girl-friends.'

The conversation gave Leane plenty of food for thought, and she was pleased when Edna accepted her offer of help with the evening meal. Chatting brightly in the kitchen and hearing all about Stan and Edna's grandchildren took her mind off Adam and the turmoil in her own heart.

At dinner Romaine sparkled. She had quite regained her good humour and optimism. Adam was to drive her up to the clinic at eight-thirty, and then spend the evening with Dr Kleber discussing case histories. Leane asked Romaine if she wanted her to go too, to help her settle in, but she shook her head.

'No. I insist that you have the evening off. Adam will drive you over first thing in the morning, and I shall look forward to seeing you then.' For a moment the smile left her face and Leane touched her hand.

'Try not to worry. Everything will be fine.'

She had an early night after taking her leave of Romaine and next morning she was up early. She found herself humming as she showered and dressed, quite looking forward to spending a morning in the theatre again, doing the work she had been trained for.

Adam was waiting when she came down and within half an hour they were on their way to the clinic. It was a perfect morning and Leane breathed deeply of the pine-scented mountain air as they drove. Adam glanced at her sideways.

'I haven't seen much of you lately. I looked for you last night when I got back from the clinic, but Edna said you'd gone to bed early.'

'I did. I felt I owed it to Romaine to be as alert as possible this morning,' she told him.

'I see. I was rather hoping to see you.'

'Oh? For any particular reason?'

He braked and halted the car at the side of the road, looking curiously at her. 'I wanted to say goodnight—to talk to you—to spend a little time alone with you. Is there anything odd about that?' He looked at her. 'Am I mistaken, Lee, or have you been avoiding me?'

She felt her colour rise. 'Avoiding you? What an idea.' She looked at her watch. 'Don't you think we should be moving?'

'In a moment.' He slid his arm along the back

of the seat. 'Leane—there's something I have to say to you——'

She bit her lip, panic rising inside her. 'But the *time*! It will look awful if we're late. You know how Romaine must be feeling.'

He grasped her shoulders. 'Lee! Will you please be quiet and listen for a minute. I have to tell you—you must know—I've fallen in love with you.'

She caught her breath and looked away, unable to meet his eyes. 'I—I don't think it's a very good idea, Adam,' she whispered. 'This isn't the time or the place.'

He shook his head impatiently. 'Please stop worrying about the time. We have plenty.'

'That's not what I mean, Adam,' she said. 'I meant that here in Switzerland—with Romaine—is not the time or the place.' She raised her eyes to his. 'You know it too, don't you?'

He regarded her solemnly for a moment. 'It's something we've no control over, Lee. One can't choose when or where these things happen.'

'Oh!' She shook her head exasperatedly. 'You're deliberately misunderstanding me, Adam!'

'For heaven's sake!' He grasped her shoulders tightly. 'I'm telling you I love you, and all you can talk about is time and place! All I want to know is—do you love me?'

Her lip began to tremble uncontrollably. 'I don't know—I don't *know*,' she said weakly.

'*Do you?*' Without giving her time to answer he pulled her close and kissed her hard. 'Oh, Lee, can't you see it's driving me mad? Can't you just tell me what you feel—whatever it is?'

She felt as though her body had turned to liquid. All her protestations, all her strength of mind evaporated as she relaxed against him. Wild happiness spread its wings within her as she whispered, 'Yes—oh yes, I love you—but it's——'

She had been going on to ask about Romaine— what their loving each other would do to her, especially at this time, but she didn't get the chance. Adam's lips came down firmly on hers again, sending all practical thoughts flying. She clung to him, responding as she had longed to, her heart beating wildly within her. At last he held her away from him, his eyes shining as he looked into hers.

'Why couldn't you let it happen like that before, darling? Why have you held me at arm's length?'

'Because I know that Romaine loves you too,' she said, giving up all attempts at subtlety. 'She considers that you belong to her—anyone can see that. If she knew about us it would upset her. I don't want to be responsible for that.'

He shrugged. 'Then we won't tell her.'

She was shocked. 'You mean go behind her back—deceive her?'

He nodded. 'Just until the operation has proved a success, of course. After that she'll be so busy with her comeback that it won't matter.'

She frowned. 'But what is your relationship with her? You seem so close—almost intimate.'

His eyes narrowed as he looked at her. 'What are you suggesting, Lee?'

She felt her colour heighten. 'Well—one can't help noticing. You're so attentive—considerate. You devote—*sacrifice* your time to her. I've heard you late at night—in her room.'

She glanced at him and saw to her dismay that he was angry. His eyes had darkened and his mouth had taken on a hardness that made her heart sink. He looked at his watch.

'You were right—we'll be late.' He switched on the ignition and the car roared to life as he pressed his foot down hard on the accelerator. Leane touched his sleeve.

'Adam—I only——'

'Never mind,' he said abruptly. 'It's obvious that you can't take me on trust, and as you pointed out, this isn't the time or the place.'

The next minute they were on the road again, speeding towards the clinic, and Leane's heart, which had flown so high just a moment ago sank despairingly.

They found Romaine in her room, prepared and sedated for the operation. Adam bent and kissed her forehead.

'Good luck, darling. I'll see you in the theatre. I must go now and get ready. Chin up.'

She smiled drowsily up at him. 'I feel wonderful, just as though I were floating on a cloud. It's funny—nothing seems to matter very much this morning.'

He patted her shoulder. 'Marvellous! See you later.' He glanced at Leane and for a moment she thought he was about to say something, but he seemed to change his mind and, turning, he left the room.

Romaine held out her hand. 'Leane.'

'I'm here.' She took it and pressed the fingers reassuringly.

'They'll be coming for me soon. You won't let me make a fuss, will you? I don't *think* I will.'

Leane smiled. 'Of course you won't. I'll be right there with you all the time. You have nothing to worry about at all.'

She looked down at the delicate face on the pillow. By all the laws of human nature she should feel jealous of this woman who so clearly loved the man she herself wanted. But as she looked down at her all she felt was pity. There must be something very much amiss with her life for her to crave so sadly for her lost youth.

The door opened and a nurse came in with a gown, cap and mask for Leane. 'Almost ready,' she mouthed. 'Is she relaxed?'

Leane nodded and the girl went out again.

'They all speak such amazingly good English,' Romaine observed, her words slightly slurred. 'Makes me feel quite ashamed that I didn't try harder at school.'

A young porter arrived with a trolley and Leane helped him to lift Romaine on to it, taking the other end as they wheeled her down the corridor to the waiting lift.

In the theatre Otto was waiting, only his kind brown eyes visible above the mask.

'Ah, there you are, Romaine,' he said jovially. He examined her face carefully, making lines with a soft pencil along the incision points. 'Nothing at all to be afraid of,' he said soothingly. 'We shall have your little job done in no time at all.'

The eyes smiled at Leane and nodded to where

she could stand at the other side of the table. He looked calmly down at Romaine. 'Now, I shall be giving you several little injections, after which you will feel nothing, then we shall cover up most of your face with towels, but do not worry. All has been done many times before.'

He glanced over his shoulder as a nurse lifted the towel covering the instrument trolley. His practised eyes surveyed it swiftly and he nodded his approval. He smiled down at Romaine. 'Without exception, all have been delighted with the result.'

He held out his hand for the syringe which was instantly placed firmly in it. Leane looked up to see Adam and Dr Helga Stein come into the theatre, gowned and masked, and take up a position above Romaine's head to watch the operation. She pressed Romaine's fingers and felt their answering pressure. She saw her bite her lip as the first of the injections was administered, but after that she seemed to relax, though the hand that lay in Leane's gripped hard as the sterile towels were placed over her face.

The Theatre Sister placed a pair of strong magnifying spectacles on Otto's nose and he held out his hand for the scalpel. At that moment there was a slight disturbance at the back of the theatre and Leane looked up just in time to see Adam leaving hurriedly, pulling off his mask as he went. She saw Dr Stein and Otto exchange glances, but the hesitation was only momentary. The next moment the first incision was made.

Leane watched, fascinated, as the skilful fingers snipped and trimmed away at the surplus skin and tissue. As he worked Otto explained to his staff in a low, unhurried voice exactly what he was doing. It was all done, cauterised and ready for sutures in what seemed to Leane a remarkably short time. She pressed Romaine's hand and was glad to feel it quite relaxed.

Otto smiled down at his patient. 'There—all is now over. We shall now put you back to bed and give you something to make you sleep. Then the nurse will pack your face with ice and keep it renewed for a few hours.'

'Ice—but why?' Romaine asked as best she could through stiff lips.

'To reduce the swelling and bruising,' Otto told her, 'and to ensure that you will be beautiful again in the shortest possible time. If you wish, you may go home this evening, but I would prefer it if you would stay one more night.'

Romaine tried to smile. 'Thank you, Otto.'

As the porter wheeled her to the lift, Otto took Leane by the arm. 'Just at first she may not be able to see very well,' he warned. 'It will be temporary only—caused by the bruising of the smaller nerves. We shall treat with drops, and of course it may not happen. This is why I did not mention it to Romaine. If it does, however, you will be prepared and will reassure her?'

'Of course, Doctor.' Leane smiled. 'Thank you for letting me stay with her. I found the operation quite fascinating.' She looked round. 'Do you know where Dr Blake is?'

He patted her arm. 'Do not worry about him. I have seen this thing happen so many times— Doctors who have done hundreds of operations turning weak at someone close to them on the table. No doubt he will be feeling very angry with himself, but it is really nothing unusual. When you see him, will you try to reassure him—and tell him I would be glad if he would lunch with me today at one o'clock, here at the clinic?'

She nodded. 'I'll pass on your message.'

She rejoined Romaine in her room just before she slipped off to sleep. A nurse sat at the bedside with a flask of ice and fresh packs. Leane pressed one of the limp hands that lay outside the covers. 'I'll be in to see you later, when you've had a rest.'

Romaine sighed contentedly. 'Thank, you dear,' she whispered.

Outside in the car park she looked around for Perdita, but the little car was not in the place where she and Adam had left her earlier, so she set out to walk back to the chalet. She had not covered more than a hundred yards, though, when she heard the sound of a car behind her and turned to see Adam drawing to a halt beside her.

He was silent as she got into the passenger seat and as he drove on he kept his eyes firmly on the road ahead.

'Romaine is fine,' she ventured. 'And Dr Kleber asked me to invite you for lunch with him at the clinic at one o'clock.' She looked at his face. It was pale and drawn, the lips set in a grim line. 'It's all right, Adam,' she said gently. 'Dr Kleber says he's seen it happen dozens of times before. It's only that Romaine is such a close friend, nothing to be ashamed of.'

He turned to look at her sharply, his face colouring. 'I am *not* ashamed,' he said, his voice ominously low. 'There's no way you can know—

no way I can make you understand what happened this morning in the theatre, or the reason for it. But I'm not ashamed of it—or of anything else in my life—now or in the past. Is that quite clear?' His eyes were hard and angry as he looked at her. She nodded, her heart heavy.

'Of course it is, Adam—I didn't mean——'

'I'm sorry for the things I said to you earlier,' he rushed on. 'It was very wrong of me to place you in what you obviously consider an impossible situation. It will not occur again.'

She bit her lip. 'Are you going to see Romaine—and lunch with Dr Kleber?'

He nodded. 'After I've taken you home, yes. I came here to work, and that's what I shall be doing from now on.'

She sank back in her seat, feeling utterly crushed. Would they never understand each other? Was she fated to make him angry? Why couldn't he be honest with her about Romaine? But most of all—why did she have to love him so?

CHAPTER EIGHT

ROMAINE came home on the morning after the operation. As Otto had warned, her vision was slightly impaired, and after the last effects of the local anaesthetic had worn off she suffered considerable discomfort. She was one of the worst patients that Leane had ever nursed.

She complained about everything—the pain and temporary loss of vision, the discomfort of the stitches. She insisted that her bed was uncomfortable, that the bath water was cold, and that Edna had forgotten how to cook. She even found fault with the weather, which had turned cloudy and dull. And the first time she looked into a mirror she was almost hysterical.

Leane found her in the bathroom which adjoined her bedroom, staring into the mirror in frozen horror.

'Oh, my God!' she wailed. 'I look terrible! How could Otto have made such a mess of it?'

Leane slipped an arm round her waist and led her back to her room. It was true that Romaine's face look far from pretty as yet. All the stitches were still in place and the swelling and bruising, though not severe, were enough to distort the delicate features almost out of recognition.

'You know Dr Kleber said you weren't to look in the mirror till he told you,' she said, thinking privately what a good job it was that Romaine had not been able to see herself when she first came home. 'It will be fine once the stitches come out and the healing can take over. A week from now you'll be thrilled, just wait and see.' Leane tucked in the covers and patted Romaine's shaking shoulder. 'Please don't cry. You'll only make matters worse. Try to have a sleep until lunchtime.'

'I don't *want* any lunch. You must be quite insensitive to suggest it!' Romaine sobbed. 'Oh, why can't you just agree that the operation is a complete failure?' Tears poured down the swollen cheeks. 'Even Adam can't face me—*he* knows. I've hardly seen him since I came home.'

It was true. Adam had spent almost all of his

time at the clinic since the operation.

'I believe he's just being tactful,' Leane said. 'He knows you hate to be seen looking less than your best. Besides that, he hates to see you upset. If you'd only try to be optimistic. You were so brave both before and during the operation.'

She sat on the bed and took Romaine's hand. 'I watched Dr Kleber operate and he made a marvellous job of it. Now you must give nature a chance to do the rest. Will you please try?'

Romaine sniffed, swallowed and sat up in bed. 'I don't want to spend all day sleeping like an old woman,' she said petulantly.

'Then read some of your scripts,' Leane suggested. 'They're all waiting, and you can see well enough now. Look, after lunch I'll do your hair for you, then you can sit up and read this afternoon. And the minute Adam comes in I'll get him to come and see you.'

Romaine nodded grudgingly. 'Pass me my dark glasses and the hand mirror.'

Leane passed them to her and she put the glasses on and studied the effect. Some of the stitches were still visible and she threw the mirror down in despair.

'They'll be out tomorrow,' Leane told her. 'You'll be surprised at how much better you'll look and feel then.'

'I hope you're right,' Romaine sighed. 'Oh, I do hope you're right.'

Outside the door Leane drew a deep breath and leaned against the wall. Sometimes it was hard to keep her patience. Romaine needed constant reassurance that all would be well and at times she could be quite cutting in her criticism of everyone—from Dr Kleber down to Edna. Adam seemed to be shirking his responsibility towards her too, but when she had tackled him about it the previous evening he had been quite short with her, giving her to understand that he would run his own life and did not welcome her interference.

Edna came up the stairs with Romaine's lunch tray and raised an eyebrow at Leane, quickly summing up the situation.

'Been difficult again, has she?' She clicked her tongue. 'You go on down and have your lunch, love. I'll take the tray in.'

Leane had been eating in the kitchen with Stan and Edna since Romaine's return from hospital. Adam had been taking all his meals except breakfast at the clinic, returning late in the evening only in time to look in on Romaine before she settled for the night. What had begun for Leane as an idyllic new experience had now turned into a difficult and tedious routine job, added to which was the trauma of her quarrel with Adam.

Stan looked at her across the table as she picked at her food in a desultory way. 'Cheer up, love. It may never happen,' he offered.

Leane forced a smile. 'Oh, it'll be all right once the stitches are out and Miss Hart can begin to see some improvement. You have to admit that it's rather a depressing time for her.'

Edna came in and closed the door firmly behind her, a determined look on her face. 'I've just given her a bit of a pep-talk,' she said. 'I think she'll pull herself together now all right.'

'What did you say?' Leane asked.

'Oh, nothing much,' Edna said as she helped

herself to potatoes. 'Just that you'd be flying off back to London if she didn't pull her socks up soon!'

The following morning Otto arrived to remove Romaine's stitches personally. He stayed for some time, taking coffee with Romaine in her room and chatting about old times; he even examined the Iceberg rose, removing the odd dead leaf and checking it for greenfly and moisture.

'I believe the first flowers will be out at about the same time that your bruises fade,' he prophesied cheerfully. 'Till then the rest will do you good, so be patient and behave yourself!' He dropped a kiss on the top of her head, glancing as he did so at the manuscripts that littered the eiderdown. 'Have you found one that you like yet?'

Romaine sighed. 'No, not really. There are several possibles, but nothing that really excites me.'

He stood up, patting her shoulder indulgently. 'If I could I would write one for you myself, my dear. As it is I shall just have to be content with making you beautiful.' He raised her fingers to his lips.

That evening Adam was home early, and in spite of the sharp retort he had given Leane when she had broached the subject, he took his dinner with Romaine in her room. Later he came into the drawing room where Leane sat reading, to tell her that Romaine was ready to be settled for the night. She stood up, replacing the book that she had been reading on the shelf.

'She's much more cheerful today,' she remarked. 'She's been through a bad time,' she glanced at him, 'and she's obviously missed your company.'

He picked up a magazine and began to thumb through it, avoiding her eyes. 'I came here to work,' he retorted. 'However much I try I can't hope to please everyone, can I?'

She ignored the implication. 'Are you enjoying your work at the clinic?' she asked politely.

'Very much.' He flipped the pages of the magazine. 'By the way, in case I forget, will you tell Edna that I'll be out for dinner tomorrow? Helga Stein and I are eating out.'

She nodded. 'Very well. I hope you have a pleasant evening.'

She walked quickly out of the room, afraid that he might see the hurt in her eyes. Did he deliberately set out to wound her? How could he be so cold and casual when he had said only a few days ago that he loved her? She took a deep breath and walked up the stairs, her head held high.

Next morning Romaine was in better spirits. Having taken a look at herself in the mirror she saw that the discoloration had faded considerably, and the swelling was reduced too. The benefits of the operation were beginning to show at last, and when Leane took in her morning coffee she found Romaine on the balcony, inspecting the little rose bush.

'Otto was right,' she said delightedly. 'Look, the buds are beginning to open. Isn't he clever?'

Leane smiled. 'I would say "clever" was much too mild a word.' She held up a package which had come by the morning post. 'I think these must be some new manuscripts from your agent. You'll have a busy day ahead.'

In the kitchen as she helped Edna with the

breakfast she told her of Romaine's cheerfulness. The other woman smiled.

'Dr Kleber's coming to dine with you all tonight. That will be the reason. I must go up in a moment and talk to her about the menu.'

The sudden talk of food jolted Leane's memory and she remembered the message Adam had asked her to give Edna.

'Oh—Dr Blake told me to tell you that he'd be dining out this evening,' she said. 'He's taking Dr Helga Stein out.'

'I see.' Edna glanced at her with shrewd eyes. 'Wouldn't have hurt him to take *you* out after the tough time you've had,' she remarked. 'What's the matter with him anyway? He's been like a bear with a sore head these last few days.'

To Leane's horror her eyes filled with tears, and Edna put down the plate she was holding and slipped an arm round her shoulders.

'There now, love. Just you take no notice of me. Always putting my foot in it, I am. I thought there was something wrong between you two. Do you want to talk about it?'

Leane shook her head. 'It's nothing really. Just that we can't seem to agree on anything and—and——'

'And you're more fond of him than is comfortable for you, eh, is that it?' Leane nodded helplessly and Edna clicked her tongue, pulling a chair out from the table and gently pushing Leane into it. 'Dear, oh dear, I was afraid of that.' She sighed. 'I've seen the way he looked at you and could've sworn——' she shook her head. 'What happened to make him turn like that, I wonder.' Her mouth hardened. 'I expect it was her ladyship! Ah well——' She picked up the tray. 'You eat your breakfast, love. I'll take Madam's tray up, then I can discuss tonight's menu with her at the same time.'

When she came down a little later she wore a puzzled look. 'Well, if that doesn't beat everything. Madam didn't know about Dr Blake being out tonight. She thought it would be the four of you. Quite put out, she was when I told her. She doesn't like that Dr Stein one little bit!'

Leane stood up. 'It will make things much easier if I take my dinner in my room,' she said. 'I'll go and tell her right away, then she won't have to worry about it any more.'

But keeping numbers even for dinner was the least of Romaine's problems that day, as time was to tell.

After lunch she sat on her balcony in the sunshine, reading one of the latest batch of scripts. She looked almost normal now. Leane had dressed her hair carefully to hide the scars behind her ears, and the dark glasses hid the rapidly fading discoloration around her eyes. Leane was just tidying the bedroom when Edna came in, looking perturbed.

'Madam has a visitor,' she whispered.

Romaine came in from the balcony. 'What is it, Edna?'

'A visitor, Madam. Someone to see you.' Edna bit her lip.

'But didn't you tell them? You know I can't see anyone yet,' Romaine said sharply. 'Who on earth is it?'

Edna looked helplessly from one to the other.

'It's—it's Mr Sands. He says he's flown over from London specially with something for you, Madam. What shall I say to him?'

Romaine's hand flew to her throat as she stared at Leane. 'Keith!' she said in a stunned voice. 'But how on earth did he get the address? I suppose John Wilton must have given it to him. Oh my God!' Her voice rose on a note of panic and Leane took her arm.

'Look, it's all right, we could say that you'd been involved in a slight accident—a fall perhaps.'

Romaine stared at her. 'Do you think we could get away with it?' She looked at Edna. 'What exactly did you say to him?'

'Just that you were resting.'

'I think you're going to have to see him,' Leane said, remembering Keith's suspicions on the night he had taken her out in London. 'After all, he *has* come a long way and he'll think it strange if you don't.'

Romaine nodded. 'You're right, of course. Oh, damn the wretched boy! I suppose I'd better get dressed.'

'Let Edna help you while I go down and explain,' Leane said. 'I'll say you were walking on one of the mountain paths when you slipped and fell, hitting your head on a rock.'

Romaine grasped her arm. 'I really hate your having to lie on my account, Leane. But bless you all the same. Just give me ten minutes.'

Leane found Keith in the drawing room where Edna had put him, and when she walked into the room his face beamed.

'Surprise, surprise, eh?'

She smiled wryly. 'You're that all right!'

He looked at her in mock innocence. 'What's all this then—aren't you pleased to see me?'

She laughed. 'Of course I am. It's Romaine. She's had a slight accident and is indisposed. You know how she hates to receive visitors when she looks less than her best.'

He frowned with concern. 'An accident? Nothing serious, I hope?'

She shook her head. 'Just a fall. Some of the mountain paths are slippery. Unfortunately she has bruises on her face.'

'Is that all?' He threw out his arms in an extravagant gesture. 'Surely I'm much too old a friend for a little thing like that to matter. Where is she? I'll soon cheer her up.'

Leane put a hand on his arm. 'Not yet. She's getting dressed. Sit down for a moment and tell me what you've been doing.'

He shook his head. 'Who wants to talk about me? You look absolutely marvellous, Lee, darling. Switzerland must suit you.' He peered round exaggeratedly. 'Er—where is the fearsome Dr Blake?'

'He's working. I told you he was going to study while he's here. He's at a clinic on the other side of the village.'

'Ah, good.' He took out his cigarette case and lit a cigarette. She eyed him thoughtfully.

'Just why *are* you here, Keith? I'm quite sure you haven't come all this way without good reason.'

He tapped the briefcase that lay on the table in front of him. 'An outline for a new play,' he said. 'I'm sure she'll love it. If she does, I could even stay on here and write it with her collaboration.'

Ten minutes later he was telling it all to Romaine as she lay on the chaise-longue in her room. 'Can't you just *see* the billing, darling?' he said excitedly. 'A comedy by Keith Sands and Romaine Hart! You might even direct it too—with my help, of course. It would be an absolute sensation!'

'It all sounds rather exhausting,' Romaine said wearily. 'And I haven't even read your outline yet.'

'Plenty of time for that,' Keith said airily. 'Take all the time you need.'

'Where are you staying?' Romaine asked.

His jaw dropped. 'Ah—well, I'd rather thought——'

'If you haven't booked in anywhere I suppose you'd better stay here,' Romaine said, her voice sharp with irritation. 'Most of the hotels will be full.'

'Wonderful!' he said rubbing his hands together. 'We can make a start on our talks right away, then, over dinner tonight.'

'Oh no we can't,' Romaine said quickly. 'I'm dining alone with an old friend this evening, and I'm not going to put him off even for you, Keith.'

Unabashed, he turned to Leane. 'That's fine by me. I'll take Leane out to dinner. I'd like that.'

Romaine and Leane looked at each other helplessly. It seemed there was no escape.

She decided to wear one of her new dresses to go out to dinner with Keith. Since Romaine's operation there hadn't been a chance to dress up. It was a floating caftan in exotic blue and green printed silk, and when she came downstairs Keith, who was waiting for her in the hall, gave a low whistle.

'Wow! You look really terrific, Lee. Look, I don't know this place at all. Where does one eat?'

She shrugged. 'I've only been to one place— The Postli.'

'Was it good?'

'Lovely.'

'Right, then that's where we'll go.'

'It's rather a long walk,' she said doubtfully as he opened the door for her, then she stopped as he pointed to Romaine's car which stood waiting outside.

'Transport by courtesy of Romaine Hart,' he said, grinning impishly. 'Well, she's not using it tonight. I thought it was worth asking.'

Leane shook her head at him. He seemed to have nerve enough for anything!

It was early in the evening and so quiet at the Postli. They sat at the bar and had a drink first while Keith looked her over with obvious admiration.

'You really are a knockout, Lee. Is that a new dress?'

'Yes.'

He pulled a face. 'I don't suppose you've had much of a chance to get out and enjoy yourself since you've been here.'

'I'm not complaining,' she said. 'After all, I'm not on holiday, I'm here to work.'

He regarded her, his head on one side. 'Your nursing training must have come in very useful.'

She felt herself colour. 'What do you mean?'

'Why, this accident of Romaine's, of course.'

He took a thoughtful sip of his drink. 'Funny, I don't see her as the mountaineering type myself.'

'You don't have to be. There are paths on the lower slopes. It was a mountain *walk*, that's all.' She shifted her position on the bar stool. The way Keith was looking at her made her uneasy.

'This place where Adam Blake is studying,' he said. 'Where did you say it was?'

'On the other side of the village—by the lake.'

'Mmm—what sort of place is it?'

'A private clinic,' she told him. 'It's run by Dr Otto Kleber, an old friend of Romaine's; that's who she's dining with tonight.'

He nodded. 'All very neat and convenient, isn't it? You know, I still can't see for the life of me where you fit into this set-up. What exactly is your function—chaperone—referee—what?'

She sighed. 'I seem to remember having this conversation with you before, Keith, and I think you know quite well that I'm here as companion to Romaine.'

He flashed his disarming smile at her. 'Of course, forgive me, Lee. Writers are notoriously nosey people. We like everything neatly labelled and docketed; no mysteries or loose ends. Shall we go and get something to eat now?'

When they were seated she looked across at him. 'Now I'd like to ask you a question, Keith. Exactly why are you here?'

He looked at her in surprise, his eyes wide with assumed innocence. 'But you know the answer to that.'

'I know about the play,' she countered, 'but is that really all?'

He hung his head like a small boy caught stealing the jam. 'You can read me like a book, can't you, Lee? You're right, there is another reason, and if you're very good I'll tell you what it is later.'

At that moment their food was placed before them and the conversation came to an end. The restaurant was beginning to fill up and the small band had begun to play. Keith smiled at Leane as he finished his first course.

'I really like this place. It has atmosphere. Will you dance?'

His arm held her close as they circled the floor.

'It's wonderful to see you again, Lee,' he told her. 'Would you believe me if I told you that you've been constantly in my thoughts since I saw you off at the airport that day?' She shrugged noncommitally and he went on: 'In fact I thought about you so much that I finally went round to ask that little flatmate of yours for your address. I thought I might write to you.'

Leane leant her head back to look at him. 'So that was how you got it! And Romaine has been blaming poor John Wilton. As for writing to me, I'm sure you have more profitable things to do with pen and paper.'

He laughed and brushed his cheek against hers. 'You've read my mind again. I thought—why not write Romaine another outline instead and take it over in person? That way I could actually see you again—the perfect excuse. And if I may say so, you seem to have grown even lovelier than I remembered you.'

Leane laughed. 'Keith! You're the worst flatterer I've ever met. It's a good job that both my feet are firmly on the ground.' As she threw back her head she suddenly caught sight of a couple who had just come in and her heart gave a lurch. The tall dark man and his stunning blonde companion were none other than Adam and Helga. Keith looked down at her with concern.

'What is it, darling? You've gone as white as a sheet.'

When she failed to answer he swung her round to follow the direction of her gaze and an impish grin spread over his face. 'Well, *well*! If it isn't the *enfant terrible* himself! And with a beautiful blonde, no less. What *would* Romaine say? Remind me to blackmail him sometime, will you?'

At that moment Adam caught sight of them and stood staring as though rooted to the spot. Quite deliberately, Keith bent and kissed Leane full on the mouth.

'Mmm—I'll bet he isn't enjoying himself half as much as I am,' he said against her hair.

Leane pushed him away feeling flustered and hot with embarrassment. 'Please, Keith—can we sit down now?'

After taking her back to the table Keith went to the bar to order a bottle of wine while Leane sank into her corner chair, trying to look inconspicuous. But their whereabouts had not gone unnoticed, and a moment later a shadow fell across the table. She looked up to see Adam looking down at her, his face dark with anger.

'What's Sands doing here?' he asked without preamble.

'He came over with a new play outline for Romaine,' she told him.

'Damned cheek! How did he know where to

find her, anyway?'

She shrugged, shrinking from admitting to him that it was partly her fault. At that moment Keith rejoined them and smiled blandly at Adam.

'Hello, there. Nice to see you again. Quite a surprise, eh? Would you and your delightful companion care to join us?'

Adam glowered at him. 'No thanks. We're just about to eat.'

'Then later, for a drink? I insist.'

Adam glanced at Leane. 'Perhaps,' he said abruptly, and moved away.

Keith sat down and looked at Leane. 'He doesn't change much, does he? Pompous as ever! Who's the girl, though? She's quite a dish.'

'She's a doctor at the clinic,' Leane told him. 'Dr Kleber's assistant.'

He nodded. 'All in the family, as it were. Well, very nice too. Tell, me, what do they do at this clinic place?'

She stared at him blankly. 'Do?'

'Yes. I mean, they usually specialise in something or other, don't they? What is it that Adam is studying so avidly that he can't study at home?'

She laughed shakily. 'Oh, I see what you mean.' She did some rapid thinking. There was no point in being cagey about it. That would be the quickest way to arouse Keith's curiosity. Anyway, he could find out easily enough from almost anyone he cared to ask. 'It's plastic surgery actually,' she said lightly. 'Dr Kleber is one of the top men in that field, a brilliant surgeon.'

Keith made no more mention of the clinic or the reason for Romaine's stay in Switzerland and as the evening wore on he became the amusing companion that Leane remembered. She began to relax at last. They danced again and Keith made her laugh with his outrageous wit. All at once she realised that in spite of everything she was enjoying herself. Once or twice she caught sight of Adam watching them, but she pretended not to notice. After all, he was with someone else, it was really none of his business what she did!

It was after eleven when Adam and Helga came across to their table. Adam introduced Helga to Keith and they sat down. The conversation was stiff and polite until Keith asked Helga to dance and they moved off towards the dance floor. When they were alone Adam looked at Leane across the table.

'I don't trust him,' he remarked abruptly. 'Surely if he had a play for Romaine he could have gone through her agent—put it in the post, even.'

Leane shrugged. 'He's ambitious. I suppose he thought he'd stand a better chance, bringing it in person.'

He glanced towards the dance floor where Keith and Helga seemed deep in conversation. As he watched Helga threw back her head and laughed. Adam frowned.

'Where's he staying?' he asked.

'At the chalet.'

'What?' He stared at her. 'You mean he invited himself?'

'Romaine invited him actually,' she told him. 'And by the way, we've told Keith that Romaine had an accident—a fall while out walking, bruising her face.'

He gave an exasperated snort. 'Oh, really! How did he know where she was, anyway?'

She bit her lip. 'I'm afraid he got the address from Bridget, my flat-mate in London.'

His face was like thunder as he picked up his glass and tossed back the rest of his drink in one gulp. Leane looked at him unhappily.

'Why don't you say what you're thinking—that you *knew* it was a mistake employing me from the start?'

'I've never said that!'

She felt her face colour. 'You didn't have to! Perhaps you even think that Keith Sands and I are in some sort of collusion and that I invited him here!' Her heart was beating fast now, and her throat was tight with unshed tears.

'For heaven's sake, Lee,' he hissed at her. 'People are looking at you!'

But the emotions she had bottled up for days would not be contained any longer. Unable to hold back the tears, she rose hurriedly and left the restaurant. In the car park she found Romaine's car; but it was locked, the keys in Keith's pocket. Tears of frustration poured down her cheeks as she stood there, helplessly rattling the door handle, till a quiet voice spoke behind her.

'Darling, don't.'

At the whispered endearment she turned and found herself in Keith's arms. Disappointment overwhelmed her as she leaned helplessly against him. Just for one moment she had thought he was Adam. She shook her head miserably.

'I'm—I'm all right.'

'What on earth did he say to you in there?' he

asked. 'It's me, isn't it? He isn't keen on me being here—is that it?'

She shook her head in a feeble protest but he was unconvinced. 'Oh, that's it all right. He's afraid I'll pinch his rich lady friend. Don't let him upset you, darling, he isn't worth it.'

He took out his handkerchief and dabbed at her cheeks. 'There, now how about a smile, eh?' She did her best and he kissed her, putting his arms around her and drawing her close. 'You really are a lovely girl, Lee,' he whispered. 'Let me make it up to you while I'm here. Let me take you out for some fun. You don't seem to have had much of that so far.'

She felt too weak to protest and even if she had tried she would not have got far, for his lips were on hers again, persuasive and sensuous. They drew apart and he opened the car door for her, tucking her into the passenger seat. Through the windscreen she saw Adam on the other side of the car park. As they drove out, the car almost brushed against him as he stood there, his face a mask of resentment. Had he seen them kiss? Or was the resentment simply because they were using Romaine's car?

CHAPTER NINE

BREAKFAST next morning was an uncomfortable meal. For reasons best known to himself, Adam did not breakfast early as he had been doing, and when she came came down Leane found the two men sitting opposite each other in frosty silence.

She said good morning to each of them and sat down.

'How's Romaine this morning?' Keith enquired.

'She's very well, thank you,' Leane replied.

'Good. I was hoping she might read my manuscript during the day and discuss it with me later.'

Adam looked up sharply. 'It wouldn't be wise for Romaine to overdo things,' he said crisply.

Keith raised an eyebrow. 'Why, is she ill? Her backers would be most disturbed to know that!'

A dull flush spread up Adam's neck. 'No, she's not ill exactly, but the—accident has shaken her and she needs rest.'

'Well, I realise that, of course. I had no intention of tiring her,' Keith said. 'In fact I was going to ask her if I could borrow Leane for the day. I thought we might take a look at Liechtenstein.'

Adam threw down his napkin and rose from the table. 'May I ask how long you intend to stay?' he asked baldly.

'I haven't decided that yet,' Keith said lazily. 'As long as Romaine and I need to iron out any difficulties that might arise.' He smiled. 'And as you pointed out, I mustn't tire her with long working sessions, must I? Anyway, I'm in no hurry.' He smiled at Leane and reached for her hand. 'I like the scenery—and the company, some of it, at least!'

Adam strode from the room without another word to either of them and Keith chuckled.

'One up to me, I think. God! What a stuffed shirt he is.'

Leane sighed. 'I wish you hadn't said we were

going out. You hadn't even asked me, and it's out of the question anyway. This is my job, Keith, and Romaine needs me.'

'Nonsense, you leave her to me,' he said confidently. 'You must have a break, you're looking very peaky and I shall tell Romaine so right away.' And before she could stop him he had left the room, heading for the stairs.

He was as good as his word. Romaine insisted that they should have their day out, and an hour later they were in the car on the road to Liechtenstein. The morning was fine, with the sun shining brilliantly out of a clear, dazzlingly blue sky. Keith was an excellent driver and Leane had good reason to be glad of it. The road climbed and dipped, twisting and turning like a snake. Often there was a sheer drop of hundreds of feet on one side which took her breath away. But the beauty of the scenery had her enthralled; the tiny villages with their pretty houses, the surrounding farms, their fields and orchards rising steeply from the roadside and the placid-faced, stone-coloured cows with their musical bells. Above all, the colour: the vivid green of the grass, the blue sky and the snow on the mountain tops.

'Such *richness*,' Leane said, taking a deep breath of the sparkling air through the open window. 'It's almost unbelievable. Oh, I *love* Switzerland!'

He smiled at her 'It certainly does things for you—makes you come alive.'

The smile left her face abruptly. His words reminded her sharply and painfully of Adam. He had said the same words to her that afternoon on the Schatzalp. He had tried to get her to confess her love for him. Why? Was it simply that he liked to feel flattered?

'Oh dear, have I said something?' Keith asked her anxiously. She shook her head.

'Just someone walking over my grave.' She forced a laugh. Today she was determined to put Adam right out of her mind.

They stopped for coffee at a delightful little spa town they passed through. There was a fountain in the little cobbled square with cups on chains from which travellers could drink the health-giving water. Afterwards they drove on, crossing the great Rhine at a point where it masqueraded as a bubbling stream, splashing over rocks and boulders. Finally they came to the wide, immaculate road which led into Liechtenstein and parked the car on the outskirts of the town in plenty of time for lunch.

They ate in the open under a striped awning at one of the town's largest restaurants and watched the people go by. Afterwards they explored the streets, admiring the beautiful buildings, the quaint shops and colourful gardens. They stared up at the Schloss, regal on its peak; a cross between a medieval fortress and a fairytale castle with its turrets and painted shutters. Eventually they bought fruit and retired to a quiet little park where they could rest and eat it.

Keith looked at her. 'Enjoying yourself?'

She smiled happily. 'Oh yes. Thank you, Keith. It's been a really lovely day.'

'What are you going to do, Lee?' he asked suddenly. 'With the rest of your life, I mean. This job is only temporary, and you say you've given up your nursing career.'

It was a sobering thought and she stopped to digest it for a moment. 'I don't know,' she answered thoughtfully. 'I'll think about it when the time comes.'

'Will you tell me the truth if I ask you something?'

She laughed. 'Of course.'

'What is really the matter with Romaine? There was no accident, was there?'

Coming out of the blue his words shocked her. She felt the tell-tale colour stain her cheeks as she stared at him, open-mouthed.

Suddenly he laughed and pulled her to him. 'What am I thinking of? Asking silly questions when I could be kissing you! We have the place to ourselves. I must be raving mad!'

She allowed him to kiss her, grateful to get out of thinking up an answer to his question.

They took their time over driving home and arrived to find that Romaine was downstairs for the first time since she had come home from the clinic. She was in the drawing room, sitting on the settee with Keith's manuscript at her side.

'Romaine! How do you feel?' Leane said, going to her.

She smiled. 'Fine. I've had a busy day. Have you both enjoyed your trip?'

Leane sat beside her on the settee and began to tell her all about Liechtenstein. She certainly did look better. The bruising had almost gone, and with the dark glasses to mask them the fine scars under her eyes could not be seen at all. No one would ever guess that she had undergone facial surgery so recently. Edna brought in the tea and Romaine poured three cups.

'So you've read the outline,' Keith ventured. 'What did you think?'

Romaine took a sip of her tea before answering: 'Frankly, darling, I'm no happier with it than I was with your first effort.'

He coloured. 'But I wrote it specially for you!'

She laughed lightly. 'Then, with respect, Keith, you can't know me very well.'

He smiled coolly. 'Well, it *is* rather a long time since you actually did anything, Romaine. I'm sorry to say it, but what you call "your kind of play" is somewhat dated now.'

Romaine's eyes narrowed as the barb went home, but she kept her composure. 'I've almost made up my mind to choose a Restoration comedy. I think I can trust the advice of my agent.'

He shrugged. 'That's all right, as long as you don't object to the inevitable comments.'

'And what might they be?'

He pursed his lips. 'Oh, you know the sort of thing—your bitchier rivals might say you were hiding behind the costume and wig—using them to disguise your age.'

In fury Romaine snatched off her dark glasses and glared at him. 'They'll say nothing of the kind! I can show my face to anyone. I *should* be able to——' She broke off in confusion and quickly replaced her glasses, with a look of frantic appeal in Leane's direction.

'Have some more tea, Keith?' Leane held out her hand for his cup. 'I'm sure that you and Romaine will come to a satisfactory agreement when you've both had more time to consider.'

But Romaine stood up. 'I'm afraid not, Leane. My mind is quite made up. I'm going to dress for dinner now. And Keith, there really isn't any more to be said on the subject, so I think it would be a good idea if you left here first thing tomorrow.'

He slammed his cup down on the table. 'Don't worry, I will! But I warn you, Romaine, I'd better not find that you've given my idea to someone else to write up for you!'

She laughed. 'Be your age, Keith.'

'I wouldn't put it past you,' he insisted. 'I haven't forgotten the mean way you stole my father's billing from under her very nose!'

Romaine waved a hand at him disdainfully. 'I've no intention of discussing ancient history with you.'

'Yes!' He gave a bitter laugh. 'Ancient history—you chose a very apt phrase there!' He got up and strode from the room. Romaine swayed, her hand to her head, and Leane was at her side instantly.

'Come and sit down and try not to let it upset you.'

'Oh dear, how unpleasant,' Romaine whimpered. 'I loathe scenes and I'm really quite fond of Keith, but I'm afraid he has a very volatile temper. He takes after his mother.' She sank on to the settee and looked up at Leane, a frown between her brows. 'Was I *very* hard on him?'

Leane shrugged noncommitally. 'Well, if his play doesn't please you there's no point in beating about the bush, is there?'

Romaine drew a long breath. 'What he said

about his father—it wasn't true, you know. Godfrey insisted that my name should be first on the bills that time. It was like him, he was a dear, generous man, but I'm afraid that his wife was jealous and made trouble over it.' She leaned back against the cushions with an exhausted sigh, and Leane shook her head.

'I shouldn't have gone out and left you today.'

Romaine waved a hand. 'Not at all, dear, you deserved a day off. I've been extremely trying since I came home from the clinic—no, don't deny it, I *know* I have. I think it must be reaction—a sort of safety valve.' She smiled. 'Anyway, I had time to read poor Keith's outline, being alone. He isn't a *bad* writer, you know, but I'd say his line was more T.V. comedy. Not my style at all.'

Leane couldn't help feeling that it would have been more diplomatic to have said this to Keith himself, but she said nothing.

Neither Keith nor Adam appeared for dinner, but Romaine came down and she and Leane ate together in the dining room, taking their coffee out on to the veranda afterwards. It was a warm, mellow evening and Romaine seemed very relaxed in spite of her earlier upset. She wore an elegant white silk jersey dress, and the beneficial effects of the operation were beginning to show now. The delicate face was smooth and young again; she looked quite radiant, and Leane told her so. She smiled happily.

'It's just as Otto promised. The bruises have faded as the blooms opened on my little rose tree.' She sighed and stretched out her arms. 'Oh, I'm so lucky! When do you think I shall be able to wear make-up again, Leane? I can't wait to experiment, and I'm so sick of these wretched glasses.'

'You'll have to ask Dr Kleber about that,' Leane responded guardedly. 'I believe Dr Stein's in charge of patients' after-care.'

Romaine pulled a wry face. 'I won't ask *her*. I don't care for the girl at all!' She glanced at Leane. 'I understand Adam took her out to dinner last night. Did he say anything to you?'

Leane shook her head. 'Keith and I ran into them at the Postli, actually.'

'Oh—and did they seem to be enjoying one another's company?'

Leane shrugged. 'I think so.'

Romaine shook her head, frowning. 'I hope they're not going to become *too* friendly. She's not his type at all.'

Leane glanced at her speculatively. Was it jealousy that clouded her face? Was her desire to renew her looks purely for the sake of her career, or did she hope to compete with younger women in attracting Adam?

Romaine retired to bed early and after a chat with Stan and Edna, Leane took a book and went to bed herself. She was not at all sleepy, and somehow she couldn't concentrate on the book. So much had happened and she felt confused: it was so difficult to know who to believe. Getting out of bed, she put on her dressing gown and sat down to write a letter to Bridget. She must ask her just how often Keith had visited the flat and what he had said.

It was almost midnight when she finally sealed the envelope. Yawning, she got up from the desk and began to take off her dressing gown, then she stopped as she heard a faint tap on the door. She listened and it came again, louder this time. Re-tying the belt of her dressing gown she went to the door and opened it a little, surprised to find Keith outside.

'Lee, I must talk to you,' he whispered urgently. 'Can I come in?'

She stared at him. 'Why—what's the matter?'

He pushed his way impatiently into the room. 'I can't talk out there, someone will hear. Close the door.'

She did as he said, turning to look at him doubtfully. He had obviously been drinking. 'What is it, Keith?' she asked.

He ran a hand through his hair. 'Look, Lee, there's going to be a hell of a row here. I'm leaving on the first train in the morning. It leaves at six. Pack your things and come with me.'

She stared at him, aghast. 'What on earth for?'

'I've told you—there's going to be trouble!'

'But it's nothing to do with me. It can't be. Sit down for a minute, Keith. You're not yourself.'

He sat down on the edge of the bed with a sigh. 'I suppose you wouldn't have a drink handy, would you?'

She poured him a glass of water from the carafe on her bedside table. He took it, smiling wryly.

'Well, suppose it's better than nothing.'

She sat by him on the bed as he drank it. 'I'm sorry about your play, Keith. I'm sure Romaine didn't mean to be unkind. It was just that you touched each other on the raw. She told me later that she thinks you're a good writer, just not on her particular wavelength, that's all.'

He gave a dry laugh. 'Oh, *very* big of her, I'm sure! I really don't know why I bothered. I only did it for my father's sake. He was once in love with Romaine, you know. She used to treat men like dirt in the old days—the old collecting instinct. She had to have every attractive man she saw, whether they belonged to anyone else or not. She enslaved them, ruined their lives, then tossed them aside like so much rubbish.'

Leane frowned. 'And did she do this to your father?'

He nodded. 'Yes. He was besotted with her. She broke up my parents' marriage and then tired of him. The tragedy was that he never stopped loving her. When I became a playwright it was his dream that I should write a play for her, but he died last year with his wish unfulfilled. That was the reason I tried so hard.'

She touched his hand. 'I'm sorry, Keith.'

He looked at her. 'Come back to London with me. This is no place for you.'

She shook her head. 'I can't. I've got a job to do.'

'It's Adam too, isn't it?' he said perceptively. 'Oh, Lee, can't you see what a fool they're making of you? Romaine plays with her young friends like pieces on a chess board. It amuses her to see people hurt. She's like some evil child. Anyway, she'd never let anyone as young and pretty as you have her precious Adam, surely you've seen that!'

His words horrified and sickened her and she stood up, turning away from him. 'It's not true, Keith. Romaine's not like you say. She's kind and generous at heart.'

He laughed bitterly. 'She must be a better actress than I thought! You'll soon see how right I am if you stay on here.' He got up and took her shoulders, turning her to look at him. 'Think again, Lee. Make up your mind to come with me before it's too late,' he said urgently.

She searched his eyes. 'What did you mean when you said there was going to be trouble—what kind of trouble? Have you done something?'

He looked into her eyes for a long moment. 'Are you coming with me?'

'No—I'm sorry, Keith, but I can't.'

'Then there's nothing else I can do. You'll just have to face the music.' He pulled her close. 'Please come, Lee. I love you, darling.'

Appalled, she tried to push him away. 'I've told you, Keith—and you know you don't love me. You're just——' But her words were lost as his lips came down on hers, crushing and bruising in their intensity. She struggled with him but he held her in a vice-like grip, crushing her to him until she could hardly breathe.

Suddenly there was a rush of air as the door was thrown open. Keith's grip on her was relaxed so abruptly that she reeled backwards and the next thing she saw was Adam's face, dark with anger as he aimed a punch at Keith's jaw.

'Get out of here!' He shouted. 'How dare you behave like this in Romaine's house! Get out at once!'

One hand to his face, Keith picked himself up from where he had fallen at the foot of the bed. 'Don't worry,' he muttered. 'Romaine Hart's house is the last place I want to be.' He turned at the door. 'You won't like it much here yourself in a few hours' time!'

Adam slammed the door on him and turned to Leane. 'Are you all right?'

She was trembling. 'Y—yes—thank you.'

He came towards her. 'What was he doing in here, anyway? Was he here at your invitation?'

'No, he was *not*,' she said shakily. 'He came to tell me he was leaving.'

'Oh, and why should that concern you?'

'If you must know, he came to ask me to leave with him,' she told him defiantly. 'Though what business it is of yours, I don't know!'

'Asked you to go with him?' The angry colour left his face. 'Why? What was there between you?'

She stared at him. '*Nothing* was between us! You *know* that!'

'I know nothing of the kind,' he said hotly. 'For all I know you might have been seeing him in London. What am I supposed to think? He comes to you late at night to tell you he's leaving—to ask you to go with him. I find the two of you in a close embrace—in your bedroom——'

'*Oh!*' Leane's heart was beating so fast that she could scarcely speak. 'Oh—how *dare* you criticise me for having Keith in my room when you—when *you*——' Before she could think about what she was doing she had raised her hand and slapped him hard across the cheek.

Shocked at her own action she stepped backwards, her hand to her mouth, staring at him in horror. For a moment he looked into her eyes incredulously, his fingers touching his cheek, then he turned abruptly and left the room, closing the door behind him with a sickening air of finality. Desolation overwhelmed her. Tears ran down her cheeks and her throat constricted as she threw herself, sobbing across the bed.

CHAPTER TEN

LEANE hardly slept at all and rose early, going down to the kitchen to make herself a cup of tea. The clock on the wall struck six as she pushed the door open and she reflected that Keith would at this very moment be leaving Mavos on the train.

'Well, you're an early bird! Couldn't you sleep?' Edna came through from the pantry, teapot in hand, but stopped as she caught sight of Leane's pale face. 'There, come and sit down, love. You look all in. What is it—trouble?' Leane nodded and she added: 'Mr Keith Sands, I'll be bound. I thought I heard something late last night.'

'He's gone,' Leane said flatly. 'On the early train.'

Edna filled the kettle and set it on the stove. 'Well, a good thing too, if you ask me. It's a funny thing, but there's always trouble where that young man is. It seems to follow him around like a great black dog.' She sat down at the table and looked again at Leane. 'What was it this time, eh?'

'Romaine didn't like his play and there was a disagreement,' Leane told her. 'Then late last night he came to my room to ask me to go back to

London with him. Dr Blake must have heard voices. He walked in and—got the wrong idea and—and——' Tears welled up in her eyes and Edna clucked sympathetically.

'There, there, don't you fret. Now that he's gone everything will be all right again, you'll see.' She poured boiling water on to the tea in the pot. 'You'll feel much better when you've had a nice hot cup of tea.'

'But that's not all,' Leane went on painfully. 'I did something *awful*. When Dr Blake made those—those insinuations, I lost my temper and I—I *hit* him!'

Edna paused in the act of pouring milk into the cups. 'You—hit him—Dr Blake?' A smile spread slowly over the homely features. 'Well, good for you, girl!'

Leane stared at her. '*Good?* You're joking!'

'Not a bit of it. You say he got the wrong idea. Well, he should have known you better. He got what he deserved if you ask me!' She pushed a steaming cup into Leane's hands.

'Maybe I should have left this morning too,' she said miserably.

Edna shook her head. 'Come on now, we'll have none of that talk. Drink up your tea, then go and have a nice hot bath. And don't worry about Dr Blake. You'll have made him stop and think a bit, if I'm any judge. As for leaving—Madam'd be lost without you. She couldn't have anyone better or more patient.'

Romaine was due to spend the morning at the clinic, where Otto was to give her an examination, and she left with Adam at nine o'clock. Leane had avoided taking her breakfast with them, making the valid excuse that she had risen early and taken hers with Stan and Edna. Romaine would not ride in Perdita, so Adam had driven her to the clinic in her own car and once they were out of the way Leane offered to help Edna with the chores. They had finished doing the breakfast dishes and Leane was about to make a start on the flowers when the kitchen door opened and Adam came in, his face grim. He looked at her.

'Can I speak to you alone a minute?'

She glanced at Edna. 'I'll finish these when I get back. I won't be long.'

In the passage he closed the door firmly. 'You'd better come through to the study, this is serious.'

Her heart beating with apprehension she followed him through the hall.

'What is it?' she asked as he closed the door. 'Has something happened? Is it Romaine?'

'Romaine is all right at the moment,' he said grimly, 'though I dread to think what will happen if she finds out.'

'Finds out *what*? For heaven's sake, will you please tell me?' Leane pleaded.

He looked at her intently. 'Listen, Lee, I'm in dead earnest and I want a truthful answer—just how friendly were you with Keith Sands?'

Her cheeks burned with annoyance. 'He was just a friend. I told you. He was good company—fun to be with, nothing more, why?'

'And how much did you tell him about why we're here?'

'Nothing—well, nothing important. Adam, why are you asking me these questions?'

He looked at her. 'I've just had a call from London. John Wilton, Romaine's agent, put a call through to me at the clinic because he didn't want to run the risk of Romaine overhearing. He tells me that the story of her operation has been leaked to the press. Apparently it's all over this morning's papers. He says there's a photograph of her as she was in her heyday and another that was taken of her a couple of years ago when she was ill. One of those candid camera jobs, snapped as she was leaving the hospital. God!' he began to pace up and down. 'If she gets to hear about it the shock will just about kill her!'

Leane bit her lip. 'It's awful—but surely you can't believe that I——?'

He spun round. 'Clearly it was Keith. He must have cabled or telephoned the story through last night. The point is, how did he know? He wouldn't dare do a thing like this unless he had positive proof. Even *he* isn't that much of a fool!'

Leane shook her head. Things were becoming clear to her now, the pieces were beginning to fall into place. This must be what Keith had meant when he had said there was going to be trouble. And he had known that she would be under suspicion, that was why he had asked her to leave with him. At least he had tried to spare her that.

As though he read her thoughts, Adam narrowed his eyes at her. 'You told me last night that he'd asked you to go back to London with him. Why should he do that?'

She stood up and faced him, her cheeks hot. 'Not because I'd aided and abetted him, if that's what you're getting at. I've no idea how he found out. All I know for sure is that it wasn't through me! Maybe he just put two and two together. He wouldn't need to be a genius to get at the truth in that way, would he?'

He let out a long breath. 'Oh, Lee, let's not get emotional about it. I'm not accusing you of deliberately letting the secret out. Sands is a very smooth operator. He has a way of getting information out of people, especially—forgive me—especially women, but he'd have to have had proof. Now think, did you say anything—anything at all?'

'No, no! I've *told* you. I was most careful at all times.' She was near to tears now.

He began to pace up and down again. 'Who else knew? There weren't many people—me, you, Stan and Edna, apart from the clinic staff. John Wilton knew, of course, but he wouldn't tell anyone. It wouldn't be to his advantage.'

Racking her brains Leane suddenly froze. She was remembering a conversation she had had with Bridget shortly before she left for Switzerland. She had a sudden vision of Bridget's face as she'd said: 'Haven't we always shared our secrets? Have I ever let you down?'

She bit her lip hard. Why, oh *why* had she let Bridget talk her into giving away Romaine's secret? If she hadn't known she couldn't have let it out. Leane knew she would never have done so intentionally, but Adam was right when he said that Keith had a way of wheedling things out of people—and he *had* been visiting the flat. He would only need to let her believe he *knew* the reason for Romaine's trip to Switzerland for her to relax and let something slip out about the operation. After that, all that would be necessary was for him to come over and confirm it for himself!

Adam looked at her. 'What is it? You've thought of something, haven't you?'

'No!' she said sharply. 'I can think of no way that Keith could have known the truth for sure.' If it really was her fault she would take full responsibility, but first she must make sure. Somehow she must get in touch with Bridget and ask her.

There was a knock on the door and Edna came in with a tray of coffee. She looked anxiously at Leane. 'I thought you could do with a cup,' she observed, looking from one to the other. 'Is anything wrong?'

'No, it's all right, Edna,' Adam said. 'The coffee's very welcome, but I'll take mine upstairs. I'll be spending the morning writing up some notes and I'll be collecting Miss Hart at lunch time.'

He took his cup and went out of the room. Edna looked doubtfully at Leane. 'Been at you again, has he?'

Leane shook her head. 'No, not really. Something has come up—a snag at home. I think I'll go down to the village when I've had my coffee. Is Stan going? May I beg a lift with him?'

'He walked down as Madam wanted the car,' Edna told her. 'He went some time ago. Is there anything I can do?'

Leane frowned. 'Of course, I forgot. No, Edna, there's nothing you can do, thanks all the same. I'll manage.'

When the housekeeper had gone she poured herself a cup of coffee and sat down to think. She must get to a phone. She daren't use the one in the house. There was an extension in his room and Adam might easily overhear. She got up and went over to the window. Outside on the drive stood both cars. Why not drive down?

She ruled out Romaine's saloon straight away, feeling sure she would never manage to negotiate its bulk and weight down the steep, winding track that led to the road. But she could manage Perdita. She had driven her once—she could do it again! Really she had no choice—she had to if she was to have the peace of mind she craved for.

She did some rapid calculations. Unless she had swapped with anyone, Bridget would have worked round to a late shift by this week, which meant she would be at the flat now. Adam's room was at the rear of the chalet, he wouldn't even hear the engine if she were careful.

Praying that he had left the ignition keys in the car, Leane picked up her bag and went into the hall, closing the front door softly behind her. A quick glance through the car window told her she was in luck, the keys were in place. She gave a sigh of relief and slid quietly into the driving seat. Starting the car, she put her into first gear and moved slowly out through the gates, her heart in her mouth. The track was narrow, but if she went slowly and kept her head she would manage it quite safely, she told herself.

The sun shone down through the trees, its brilliant rays flashing intermittently into her eyes, making visibility difficult, but she rounded the first bend quite easily and began to pick up speed a little. She came to the next bend, a sharper one, and began to ease the car round it. Once more the sun flashed blindingly into her eyes. She blinked, then she saw them: a group of young climbers walking straight towards her.

They seemed to have come out of nowhere. One minute the track was empty—the next they were there and there seemed no way she could possibly miss hitting them. She saw their startled faces as she pressed her foot down hard on the brake pedal, at the same time twisting the wheel to the right in a desperate effort to avoid the young people. The car careered crazily across the grass verge and plunged over the edge, the tyres skidding on the slippery pine needles, then it hit a tree and came to a shuddering stop, lurching over sideways. To Leane it seemed that the world was turning upside down. She hurtled out of the door and on down the slope, somersaulting and rolling, till at last something struck her a sickening blow on the head and she lost consciousness.

She could only have been unconscious for a few seconds. When she came to herself it was to see a young man with fair hair peering anxiously down at her and asking her a question in German. Then she heard another voice, a familiar one shouting, 'Let me see her—I'm a doctor,' and the next moment Adam's face swam above her.

All she could think of was the car—Perdita. Had she wrecked it? Adam would be furious. She moistened her dry lips and whispered:

'Adam—I'm so sorry—your car.'

But he shook his head as he knelt beside her. 'Don't try to talk.'

Very gently he examined her, questioning the young people as he did so, then, satisfied that nothing was broken, he lifted her carefully and carried her back to the track. He assured the white-faced youngsters that no harm was done and they were not to blame, then he carried Leane back to the chalet and into the drawing room, where he laid her gently down on the settee.

Tears began to slide down her cheeks. 'Oh, Adam—your lovely car! I'm so sorry.' But he shook his head as he sat down beside her and took her hand, his face white and drawn.

'Do you think I give a damn for the car as long as you're all right? Oh, Lee darling, you're all that matters to me, don't you know that?'

He drew her into his arms and held her close as she cried, letting the tears flow in warm relief. He stroked her hair. 'When I heard the crash I knew somehow that it was you. I thought maybe I'd driven you too far and that you were running away from me. I couldn't get to you fast enough—and all the time I was dreading what I might find. Thank God you're safe!' He looked down at her, his eyes searching hers. 'You *are* all right, aren't you, darling? And where were you off to in such a hurry?'

She nodded, gently fingering the bump on the side of her head. 'I'm fine except for this—but I have a confession to make. One other person *did* know about Romaine's operation: my flat-mate, Bridget. I know I shouldn't have told her but I didn't think it could possibly matter at the time. She'd never even heard of Romaine Hart. But since then she's got to know Keith, and he's been visiting her at the flat. Perhaps he wormed the information he wanted out of her. That's where I was going. I had to get to a telephone and find out. You see, it may all be *my* fault!'

'Poor darling.' He took her in his arms again and rocked her to and fro. 'What a day this is becoming.' He smiled down at her. 'No need for you to worry any more. Just after you left the house I had a call from Helga at the clinic. She'd heard of the press leak from Otto and she confessed that she told Keith. It seems that he took her out last night. Somehow he led her to believe that he was in Romaine's confidence and she realises now that she said enough to give the whole game away. The poor girl was terribly upset about it, but it can't be helped now. With devious people like Keith around no one's private life is sacred.'

She stared at him, relief flooding through her. 'I couldn't believe that Bridget would have given him any information. I know it doesn't really improve matters, but I'm so glad it wasn't my fault!'

He kissed her and pressed her gently back against the cushions. 'You must take it easy for the rest of the day. You've had a nasty shock. I'd be happier really if you'd let me take you up to the clinic for a check-up.'

But she shook her head. 'I'm fine. And I'd rather Romaine didn't find out about this. There's enough trouble without adding to it.'

At that moment the door burst open and a white-faced Edna stood on the threshold. 'What's happened?' she demanded. 'I've just seen the car—is she hurt? Oh, my dear lord!'

Adam calmed her down, explaining as best he could what had happened while she stood shaking her head and clucking anxiously.

'I was out at the back with some washing. Honestly, I've only to turn my back in this house for something terrible to happen! Now are you sure you're all right?'

'I'm quite well, really,' Leane assured her. 'And I'd rather Miss Hart didn't hear about the accident. You see——' She looked at Adam. 'Don't you think Stan and Edna ought to know?'

He nodded. 'There's been rather an awkward development, Edna. Somehow the news about Miss Hart's operation has been leaked to the press in London. Today's papers carry the full story, apparently.'

Edna gasped. 'Oh! That's torn it! Whatever will Madam say if she hears about it? Thank goodness we don't get the English papers here until they're two days old. Maybe we can find some way to keep it from her.'

Adam shook his head. 'I'm afraid she'll have to know. I can think of no way we can spare her from it; all we can hope for is that she'll take it philosophically. But I'd be glad if you'd say nothing about it till I tell you.'

Stan's voice floated to them from the hall and Edna started. 'He'll have seen the car on his way home from the village. He must be wondering what's happened. I daresay he'll give you a hand to get it back on the road, Doctor.'

'I'd be very grateful for his help.' Adam turned to Leane as the door closed behind Edna. 'How are you feeling now?'

She smiled at him as she sat up and swung her legs to the floor. Her head ached and she still felt shaky, but she had never been happier in her life.

Adam had clearly shown her that he loved her this morning, in spite of all that had passed, and she knew that she would have suffered a dozen accidents to see him look at her as he was doing now.

'I feel wonderful,' she replied truthfully. She stood up and slipped her arms round his neck. 'I thought you'd be furious about the car.'

He regarded her solemnly. 'I've given you a pretty rough time, haven't I? I haven't meant to. It's just that nothing seems to have gone right—there's so much I have to explain to you and can't——' He broke off, looking into her eyes. 'Can you trust me, Lee—just for a little longer?'

She nodded. 'Of course, if you ask me to.'

He smiled at her wryly. 'I suppose you realise you drove me mad with jealousy when I saw you with Keith Sands? But it made me realise that I expected you to take too much on trust, expected you to accept what I couldn't myself. This evening we'll have a talk to Romaine; tell her how we feel, eh?' His eyes searched hers and all she could feel was the ache of her love for him, closing her mind to all the unanswered questions that rose to her lips.

'Will she mind?' she whispered.

He shook his head. 'Everything will be fine, you'll see, my darling.' He kissed her long and deeply and her arms closed round him, her heart soaring with happiness. It was some time before either of them spoke, then Adam said reluctantly:

'I'd better go and see if Stan can help me with Perdita, then I must fetch Romaine from the clinic.' He kissed the tip of her nose. 'Will you be all right?'

She took his hand firmly. 'I'll come to the clinic with you, then we can break the news of the press leak to Romaine together.'

He looked doubtful. 'I'd feel happier if you rested for a while.'

'How can I rest when I feel this happy?' she laughed.

When they joined Stan they found that he had already assessed the state of the car and, seeing no hope of getting her back on to the road without mechanical help, he had telephoned to one of the local garages. The breakdown vehicle arrived promptly and a cheerful mechanic promised to have the damage repaired as soon as he could. Leane watched with a crestfallen expression as the little car disappeared down the track, her front wheels ignominiously in the air. Adam took her hand and squeezed it.

'Don't look so worried, darling, it's only a broken windscreen and a few dents. That's nothing to old Perdita. She's had far worse.'

But Leane shook her head. 'I shouldn't have taken her without asking.' She looked up at him. 'You won't tell Romaine, will you?'

He smiled. 'We'll let her think Perdita is in the garage for a service.' He took her shoulders, turning her to face him. 'It could have been so much worse, Lee. But as it is, it's given me much more than it's taken from me. It was the best thing that could have happned—apart from this.' He kissed the bump on her head. 'Now, shall we go and collect Romaine?'

When they arrived at the clinic Romaine was ready to leave, looking radiant after being pronounced quite healed and given the go-ahead to wear make-up. She got into the back of the car with Leane while Adam stood talking earnestly with Otto on the steps.

'I just can't wait to throw these horrid glasses away and get out my make-up box again,' Romaine said, her eyes sparkling.

Leane's heart sank as she looked at the happy face. Her smile would soon vanish when she heard the news she and Adam had to break to her. Perhaps she wouldn't even be fit for that talk Adam had said they'd have with her this evening.

By the time they arrived back at the chalet, Romaine had sensed that something was wrong.

'You're both very quiet,' she said as the car drew to a standstill outside the door. 'I hope you haven't been quarrelling.'

Adam turned to her. 'Something has come up, Romaine. I think we'd better have a talk. Shall we go inside?'

She looked from one to the other, the colour fading from her face. 'Oh dear, you look so serious. I have an idea I'm not going to like this. Couldn't we have lunch first?'

But Adam was already opening the door, holding his hand out to her. In the drawing room he closed the door carefully and cleared his throat, while Romaine and Leane sat down on the settee.

'Please, Adam, will you tell me at once what it is,' Romaine demanded. 'I can't stand the suspense another minute! Is someone dead? Has something happened at home?'

Adam knew she was thinking of Heathridge House and her beloved horses, not her public, but all the same he nodded.

'Yes, at home, Romaine. I'm very sorry to have to tell you this, but the news of your operation has somehow been leaked to the press. It's in today's papers.'

There was a stunned silence as she digested the news. She pulled off the dark glasses impatiently, frowning down at them for a moment, then she got up and walked to the window.

'I suppose I should have known,' she said at last. 'The public isn't as gullible as it once was. And anyway, the public I *had* is no more. I hadn't really faced that fact.' She turned to them, a bright smile on her face. 'What I've had done is almost routine nowadays. Hundreds of women have it, I learned that from Otto. I suppose I should be flattered that my little operation commanded so much interest. After all, they say that any publicity is better than none.' Her smile faded. 'It was Keith, of course?'

Adam shook his head. 'We don't know that for sure, Romaine.'

But she waved a hand dismissively. 'Oh, of course it was. It's what I would have expected. The boy is his mother all over again, he did it out of pique.' She sighed and held out her hands to them. 'Thank God I have some true friends. Now, let's have lunch, shall we?'

It was later that afternoon when the three of them were taking tea on the veranda that Edna came through to say that there was a call for Adam from London. He went to take it in the study and reappeared some minutes later with a slightly apprehensive look on his face. He drew his chair up close to Romaine's and sat down.

She looked at him anxiously. 'Oh dear—not

more bad news! I don't think I could stand it.'

He smiled reassuringly. 'Not bad news exactly, though it rather depends on the view you take of it. That was John Wilton. It seems that since this morning's papers came out he's been inundated with offers for you.'

Romaine's colour rose. 'Offers? What kind of offers?'

He paused and took a deep breath. 'There have been two from T.V. chat shows, one from a radio programme for women and another from a top women's magazine,' he told her.

'I see.' Her colour drained as she realised what he was trying to tell her. 'Their interest in me is purely medical. I'm to be the modern equivalent of a freak in a sideshow!'

Adam smiled wryly. 'Oh come on, Romaine. That's rather putting the worst light on it. This sort of thing always arouses interest. Think of the heart transplant cases that are interviewed by the media. Think how good it will be for the box-office.'

Romaine stared at him angrily. 'Do you honestly imagine that I want the public to buy tickets for my play out of—of *morbid curiosity*?'

'But they wouldn't,' Leane put in, 'if they'd seen you on T.V. first. You're living proof of how successful the operation can be, and yours is a wonderful story of courage and optimism. Your comeback would be the culmination of all that.'

Romaine bit her lip. 'All the same, it wasn't exactly what I had in mind.' She sighed. 'This really does put an entirely different complexion on things, doesn't it?'

Adam patted her hand. 'It does, but it could be

turned to your advantage. Why not think it over, Romaine? Sleep on it, and perhaps give John a ring tomorrow and have a talk.' He glanced at Leane. 'While we're on the subject of talks, there's something Lee and I want to speak to you about.'

But Romaine was on her feet. 'Not now, Adam. I want to go up to my room and be quiet for a while. I haven't yet had time to get used to the idea of being a walking exhibit.' She turned to them at the door, relenting a little. 'You can come and talk to me while I'm dressing for dinner, if you like.'

When she had gone Adam gave an exasperated little snort and Leane looked at him reprovingly. 'Maybe we should leave it for now. Don't you think she's had enough shocks for one day?'

He laughed gently at her. 'Shocks? I hope that what we have to tell her won't come into *that* category.'

But Leane couldn't help feeling that it would.

Adam insisted that the best idea would be for him to see Romaine first alone, so, when he tapped on the bedroom door at seven o'clock that evening just as Leane was zipping her into her dress, she withdrew quietly, leaving them together.

In her own room she paced up and down, too nervous to keep still. Vainly, she tried to imagine the conversation taking place in Romaine's room at this very minute. She re-did her hair, applied fresh lipstick, examined her nails. Finally, unable to bear the suspense any longer, she decided to go and lend her support.

Outside Romaine's door she hesitated. Adam

had said that he would come and fetch her when he was ready, maybe she should have waited. Inside all seemed ominously quiet. The door was ajar and she raised her hand to knock. Then she heard Adam's voice speaking softly. Through the opening of the door she could see the dressing table and, reflected in the mirror, she saw Romaine sitting on the bed, Adam beside her, his hand clasping hers. As his words reached her ears she froze into immobility——:

'You know very well what you mean to me, Romaine. You know I'd do anything in the world to save you from unhappiness. I know what you've been through and ever since I realised the truth I've sworn to make it up to you. To me you've always been the dearest person in the world—even before we were together. I love you very much. I think I've proved that much to you.'

Leane's hand flew to her mouth. Her heart was hammering so loudly she felt sure that they must hear it. What kind of game was Adam playing? Whatever it was, it was cruel. How could he pretend to love two women at the same time?

At that moment he looked up and caught sight of her reflection in the mirror as she stood whitefaced in the doorway. Slowly he stood up, his face contorting in an agony of confusion, then, looking helplessly from one to the other, he walked out of the room, brushing past Leane without a word.

She stood there in the open doorway, too stunned to move, while Romaine looked back at her through the mirror.

'Come in, Leane,' she said calmly.

Leane walked into the room and closed the door. The time had come for a reckoning. Now all the cards must be put on the table—however painful it was. But when she looked at Romaine she found that she was smiling gently.

'Please, child, don't look like that,' she said. 'So you and Adam love each other? Would you be surprised if I were to tell you that it's precisely what I'd been hoping for?' She patted the bed beside her. 'Come and sit down, dear. We must have a talk. In spite of what I've just said I won't pretend that it doesn't feel strange. It's quite an occasion, after all, when a mother loses her son to another woman!'

CHAPTER ELEVEN

LEANE stood staring speechlessly. Had she heard right? Was she dreaming? Romaine stood up and crossed the room to her, putting her arms around her and kissing her cheek.

'Oh dear, is it *such* a shock? You look quite shattered. But I suppose I should take it as a compliment.'

'But how? I don't understand,' Leane said, shaking her head. 'I thought—it seemed——'
Romaine held up her hand.

'You shall hear the whole story.' She rang the bell by the fireplace to summon Edna. 'You and I shall dine up here alone tonight. Adam must eat in solitary splendour for once. All this is going to take some time, and I want to be sure you understand everything clearly. I owe you that much.'

Edna looked puzzled at Romaine's unusual request, but when she had been assured that no one was ill she agreed readily and soon reappeared with a cloth and cutlery, quickly laying the low table before the fireplace, while Stan followed behind with a laden tray. When at last they were alone and seated at their meal, Romaine began:

'I was just twenty-two when Adam was born. My career was just beginning to flower: I was doing what were known as "number three tours" of West End successes. Those are the ones that go round the provincial theatres. It was a wonderful life and I loved it. I'd acquired a good agent and he was beginning to get some quite promising offers for me. Then the blow fell—I discovered that I was pregnant.'

She sighed. 'At first it seemed like the end of the world, but after some thought and quite a bit of planning the solution seemed obvious. I arranged to take the three final months off, have the baby and have it adopted. My agent was sympathetic. He agreed to cover for me—keep the whole thing quiet.' She smiled wryly. 'Remember, the public hated any whisper of promiscuity in those days. Well, my spirits rose again. Everything was to be plain sailing. Then Adam was born, and when I held him in my arms I knew that nothing on this earth could ever make me part with him.' Her eyes were misty as she smiled reminiscently.

'So what did you do?' Leane prompted.

Romaine took a deep breath. 'Well, I was lucky. I'd made some charming friends while I was on tour. They lived in a large town in the Midlands and I'd stayed there with them when I was playing the theatre there. They were childless—their own son had died when he was very small, and they were unable to have another baby. Apart from my agent they were the only other people I'd told about my pregnancy, and they'd very kindly offered to let me stay with them while I recovered from the birth.

'When they saw Adam they were as enchanted with him as I was. We discussed it and decided mutually that the best thing for Adam would be a foster home. To my great delight my friends agreed to be his foster parents, though in actual fact they all but adopted him. They were the ones who earned the title of Mummy and Daddy.'

'That must have hurt you a little,' Leane said.

Romaine nodded. 'It did, but it was better than losing him altogether. Besides, my agent made certain conditions. When he first learned that I intended to keep the baby he was furious. He threatened to drop me if any whisper of it got out. So John and Diana Blake brought Adam up, and had his name changed to theirs by deed poll. I saw him as often as I could and sometimes I took him away for the holidays.' She smiled reminiscently. 'He was such a dear little boy and then later, so clever. I was so proud when he told me he wanted to become a doctor.'

'He told me once that he worked for it without any help at all,' Leane said.

'It's quite true, he did,' Romaine agreed. 'That was partly why, when I decided to come here to Otto's clinic, I invited Adam too. I felt it would be my contribution to his career. I had so little hand in his education, you see.'

Leane was puzzled. 'But why is it still not generally known that Adam is your son?' she asked.

Romaine looked uncomfortable. 'After all these years it might be rather embarrassing, don't you think? We talked about it and both decided that we neither of us had anything to gain. Knowing ourselves was all that mattered, we thought.' She smiled wryly. 'Oddly enough, it never occurred to me that people might take Adam for *more* than a friend of mine.'

Leane felt her colour rise and Romaine nodded.

'It's all so clear now, the way it must have looked to everyone—including you, my dear. How hurt and bewildered you must have been! And poor Adam couldn't correct your misapprehension without consulting me first.' She touched Leane's hand. 'I hope you can forgive us, dear.'

'Of course, there's no question of that,' Leane said. But there was still something she was burning to ask. 'Supposing—just supposing——' she began, groping for the words. 'I mean—if Adam's father had married you——'

'He didn't know,' Romaine put in quickly. 'I couldn't tell him. His career was promising too, and so much more important than mine. Besides, by the time I knew that I was pregnant he'd already left the country. I promised myself that no one should ever know his identity.' She sighed. 'I think perhaps that was the hardest decision of all.'

'But didn't you feel he had a right to know?'

Leane asked. 'Didn't you feel that he would have *wanted* to know his son?'

Romaine sighed. 'Looking back, I think he would, but at the time things looked different. You see, he was betrothed to someone else at the time. I felt certain he would marry her and I couldn't wreck it for him.'

Leane frowned. 'Forgive me for saying so, but I think he behaved rather badly. Perhaps you and Adam were better off without him!'

But Romaine shook her head. 'It wasn't quite like that. The girl he was betrothed to was a childhood friend. It was the choice of their parents, a foregone conclusion. He wasn't in love with her.'

Leane fell silent as she considered all the facts. A suspicion was beginning to emerge in her mind, but before she had time to examine it, Romaine said:

'And now I have to make a confession to you, Leane. I've been quite shamefully matchmaking ever since I first engaged you. You see, Adam has devoted so much time to me ever since he knew of our real relationship: I told him the full story just as I've told it to you. I knew I ran a risk. I thought he might turn from me, seeing me as a selfish, unnatural mother, but the opposite happened. He saw the sacrifice and heartache I'd suffered and he has been trying hard to make it up to me ever since.

'At first it was wonderful to feel so cosseted, but then I began to worry about him. He seemed to have so few friends. I wanted to see him fall in love and become happily married. I was at my wits' end, then I hit on the idea: I would employ a young woman to accompany us on this trip. And I would let Adam himself do the choosing!'

Leane laughed. 'It almost failed hopelessly. We loathed each other to begin with!'

Romaine joined in her laughter. 'Oh, I always feel that's a *very* good sign. It didn't escape my notice.' She smiled. 'Have I made everything clear to you now? If you have any questions do ask them.'

Leane bit her lip. 'Does Adam know who his father was?'

Romaine shook her head. 'He repects my silence on that.'

'But don't you think he might want—*need* to know?'

Romaine looked at her for a long moment, then she sighed. 'Of course, you're quite right. He should know really. But it could be very difficult—very difficult indeed.'

Leane reached out and touched her hand. 'Romaine—I hope you'll forgive me, but I believe I've guessed.' Romaine raised her eyes slowly to hers and she went on: 'All that you've told me points to one man. It's—Dr Kleber, isn't it?'

Tears began to run down Romaine's cheeks as her lips framed the word 'yes'.

'And they really never knew—either of them?' Leane asked incredulously.

Romaine shook her head, fumbling for a handkerchief, 'He never married after all. All those wasted years. Take it from me, Leane, no career is worth it. What a fool I was!'

'But is it too late?' Leane asked. 'He's obviously still devoted to you.'

'How would I ever begin to explain now?'

Romaine asked. 'After all these years? Otto might be angry—might feel I'd cheated him.'

'They like each other so much—they get along so well,' Leane ventured. 'It seems such a pity.'

But Romaine was adamant. 'Much better leave things as they are. I know you'll respect my wishes on this, dear. Believe me, it's the best way.' She smiled. 'And now I think Adam will be waiting for you—impatiently, if I know my son. Why don't you run along to him?'

Leane looked at her anxiously. 'Are you sure you're all right? You've had quite a day.'

Romaine rose and kissed her cheek softly. 'Bless you, no. I'm just rather tired. I'll have an early night. You two go off and celebrate, and I shall look forward to hearing about your plans tomorrow.'

When she came downstairs Leane saw that Adam was on the veranda where Edna had brought him his coffee. For a moment she stood unobserved, watching him, noticing now how like his father he was: the same dark expressive eyes, the same stature and build too. How proud Otto would be if he only knew. But after all the years of sacrifice, Romaine must be allowed the last word, she supposed.

As though he sensed her standing there, Adam turned and rose from his chair. As she walked towards him his eyes searched hers.

'Well—she told you?'

She nodded. 'It was a surprise.' She took the hands he held out to her. 'So much is clear to me now, Adam. I'm sorry. I should have had more trust. I should have known there was an explanation.'

He drew her to him. 'How could you have guessed? We're a pretty unlikely pair for mother and son. Perhaps now you can understand how I felt that morning in the theatre. When I saw Romaine on the operating table, being so brave.' He shook his head. 'When I thought of what was about to take place I——' he smiled wryly. 'Well, you know the rest.'

She stood on tiptoe to kiss his cheek. 'Of course.'

He looked down at her. 'You don't mind—about my questionable origins?'

She slid her arms around his neck. 'All I mind about is that the misunderstandings are cleared up. Nothing else matters to me, Adam.'

He kissed her, suddenly laughing with relief. 'We must celebrate. Where shall we go?'

'The Postli,' she said decisively.

'Right—the Postli it is—oh——' He stopped suddenly. 'I keep forgetting, I've no car.'

She linked her arm through his, looking out at the evening sky, twinkling with stars. 'Let's walk,' she said. 'It's such a beautiful night. A night I shall want to remember.'

As it happened it was a night to remember, but neither of them realised just how memorable it was to be. They danced at the Postli till late then set out on the walk home. The last stretch of the mountain road was steep and they paused frequently to catch their breath. Some thoughtful authority had placed benches at intervals for this purpose, and as they sat looking at the mountains and the night sky, marvelling at the brilliance of the stars, Adam said:

'I haven't asked you the most important question of all yet, Leane.' He took her face between his hands. 'I love you very much, darling. Will you marry me?'

'Of course I will,' she responded huskily.

He kissed her and drew her head on to his shoulder. 'What do you want our life together to be, darling?' he asked.

She sighed happily. 'Well, I'd like children—at least four.' She glanced up at him. 'But first——' She hesitated and he looked down at her.

'Go on—first?'

'I was going to say that first I'd like to go back to nursing for a while. I feel it's something I've left undone—a debt unpaid, as you once said yourself.'

He winced slightly. 'How pompous and stuffy I must have seemed.'

She laughed. 'You did, but you were right, nevertheless. I think I'm ready to go back now.'

'Perhaps you could apply for a job at Great Horton Street,' he suggested. 'Then we could be together.'

She looked at him. 'You won't be staying on here, then?'

He sighed uneasily. 'It's a wonderful experience, of course, working with a brilliant surgeon like Otto. But if I'm going to specialise in plastic surgery I want to be able to help less fortunate people, not just the wealthy. Don't think I'm criticising. Otto has been so generous to me, given me so much of his time. I've learned more in the few weeks I've been here than I could have done in months at home. I can't help feeling it's unfair, feeling as I do. I wish there were some way I could pay him back.'

Leane's heart quickened. If Adam only knew of his true relationship with Otto Kleber he would feel differently. But she had given her word. There was nothing she could do about it.

'You've worked very hard too,' she pointed out. 'I'm sure that Dr Kleber has been grateful for your help. And he wouldn't expect you to commit yourself at this stage.'

He lifted his shoulders. 'Well, we'll see. It's something I must sort out soon, especially as I'm to have a wife to support soon.' He looked down at her with a twinkle in his eyes. 'But, as you would say—this isn't the time or the place.'

He drew her close, laughing down at her teasingly. 'With the stars and moon shining down like this, who wants to talk about work?' He kissed her, tenderly at first, then more urgently till her senses swam dizzily. After a while he tipped her chin with one finger till her eyes looked into his.

'How long before we can be married, Lee darling?'

She shook her head. 'We must wait until we get back to London, I suppose. There are so many people who'll want to wish us well.'

He frowned. 'Would they be as disappointed as all that?' he asked, holding her close. 'The end of the summer seems an eternity away. I'm not at all sure I can wait that long.'

She smiled tenderly, tracing the strong line of his jaw with her fingertip. 'Maybe they'd forgive us. We could always give a party when we got home.'

His eyes shone. 'We could be married in the

little English church by the lake—with Romaine and Otto as witnesses.'

'Would you like me to ask Helga to be a bridesmaid?' she laughed. 'You'll never know how jealous I was of her the other night at the Postli.'

'Of Helga?' he stared at her in astonishment. 'And there was I hardly able to keep my hands off Keith Sands's throat!'

They laughed together, then kissed, then laughed again, getting up at last reluctantly from the bench and setting out on the last leg of the walk home, arms around each other's waists, their eyes as starry as the night sky.

It was as they rounded the last bend in the track and came in sight of the chalet that they saw Perdita standing on the drive. They stopped and looked at each other, hardly able to believe their eyes. Hurrying over to the little car, Adam inspected her thoroughly: all the repairs had been expertly carried out. Perdita was as good as new.

'Isn't it wonderful?' Leane smiled, walking round the car delightedly. 'I can't tell you how relieved I am. Aren't you pleased, darling?'

He hugged her. 'This must be my lucky day. She's perfect again. But I don't understand. Whoever worked on her must have slogged for hours without a break. I wonder if Edna is still up? Perhaps she can shed some light on it. She might have spoken to the man who brought Perdita back.'

They found Edna in the kitchen and she told them that the garage manager had delivered the car in person only half an hour ago.

'He was such a nice man, a Mr Heeb,' she told them. 'Stan and I were having a bedtime drink and we asked him to join us. He was telling us that a year ago his only son was badly injured in a motor-bike crash. Dr Kleber put him right, operated on his face and hands, which were badly burned, and only charged a very small fee. As soon as he knew that you were a doctor at the clinic he was determined to do the best and quickest job he could. He said he could never do enough to repay the debt he owes.'

'Did he leave the bill?' Adam asked.

Edna shook her head. 'He said there was no charge. He'd only been waiting for an opportunity like this. He said he hoped you'd be pleased.'

'I am, but I can't accept the work for nothing,' Adam protested. 'He doesn't owe *me* anything. I wasn't even here when his son was treated. I must find him and explain.'

'He only left about ten minutes ago,' Edna said, 'and he said he was going back to the garage to tidy up.'

Adam started towards the door. 'I'll go down there straight away,' he said.

'Oh, Adam, why not leave it till the morning?' Leane said. But he was already halfway through the door.

'No, I'll go now. I can't let the man work all day and half the night for nothing. It won't take long.'

As the door closed behind him Edna shook her head, smiling at Leane. 'Well now, I don't have to ask if *your* problems are sorted out. One look at your face is enough.'

Leane laughed. 'Yes, everything's fine now. If I tell you something, will you keep it to yourself for a few hours?'

Edna nodded, looking at her expectantly. 'Of course I will, love, though I think I've already guessed what it is.'

'Adam and I are engaged—probably getting married quite soon, maybe even here in Mavos,' Leane told her breathlessly.

The housekeeper hugged her soundly. 'Oh, I'm so glad for you both, lovey.' Her eyes twinkled. 'What did I tell you? It was that clout you gave him that did the trick, I'll bet. Do you know, I remember the time when my Stan——'

Her words were cut short by the frantic buzzing of the indicator panel over the door and she looked up in concern. 'That's Madam's bell. I thought she was asleep hours ago. I hope nothing's wrong!' Together they hurried towards the stairs.

As soon as they opened the door it was obvious that Romaine was having some sort of attack. She was out of bed and standing by the fireplace where she had gone to press the bell. She stood staring speechlessly at them, one hand to her throat, her face deadly pale and her lips bluish. Leane ran to her and slid an arm round her waist.

'It's all right, Romaine. I'm here,' she said reassuringly. 'Are you in any pain?'

Romaine nodded, gasping, and Leane helped her across to the bed, piling the pillows behind her with Edna's help.

'She has some capsules for the pain,' Edna said, rushing to the dressing table drawer to get them. But Leane shook her head.

'Not this time, Edna,' she warned quietly. She undid the collar of Romaine's housecoat and went to the bathroom for a towel to wipe the perspiration from her face, trying all the time to remain as calm as possible. She didn't like the look of Romaine at all; her colour and condition brought back sharply the memory of the night in Casualty and the patient who had died of a heart attack.

She looked up at Edna's white face. 'Supposing you make us all a cup of tea, Edna?' she said, the brightness of her own voice ringing false in her ears. As Edna moved off she followed her to the door.

'Ring Dr Kleber and ask him to get here as soon as he can,' she whispered urgently. 'I'm afraid she's having an angina attack. That was why I didn't want her to have one of the capsules, they reduce the blood pressure. Oh, if only Adam hadn't gone out!' She closed the door on Edna's scurrying figure and turned to Romaine with a forced smile.

'There, you'll soon be feeling better now.' But the words were hardly said when Romaine gave a gasp and slipped to one side. Immediately Leane sprang into action. Working as quickly as she could she pulled the limp body to the floor. Checking, she confirmed her suspicion that there was no pulse and, pulling the housecoat open, she began cardiac compression. Grabbing a pillow from the bed, she pushed it under Romaine's neck and positioned her head, then she began mouth-to-mouth resuscitation.

While she worked a dozen thoughts went through her head. Romaine *must* recover. She couldn't let her die. Adam would never forgive her. For this to happen just when they were all so happy!

She worked with all the strength and determination that was in her—compression—inhalation—pause and observe—— All the time her own heart was beating urgently, almost as though willing the silent one to re-start. At last she was rewarded by the movement of Romaine's chest and, fingers on the carotid pulse in her neck she felt the familiar throb, weak, but unmistakable. Almost crying with relief, she continued to breathe into Romaine's mouth, giving her the vital oxygen from her own lungs while she recovered.

When she saw the eyelids beginning to flutter she pulled the eiderdown from the bed and tucked it warmly round the prone figure on the floor, adjusting the pillow and turning Romaine's head to one side. With overwhelming relief she watched the colour return to the skin, and finally Romaine opened her eyes to look bemusedly up at her.

'W—what happened?' she whispered. 'Did I faint?'

'Yes, but you're fine now. Just lie there and rest.' Leane took her hand.

At that moment the door opened and Adam came in. She saw from his face that he realised what had happened, but he was careful to keep the concern from his eyes as he helped Leane to lift Romaine back into bed.

'I'll go and get some hot bottles,' Leane said to him as she tucked in the covers.

Outside the door she leaned against the wall, her eyes suddenly filling with tears of thankfulness, and when she felt a light touch on her arm she was surprised to see Otto standing there. His eyes looked anxiously into hers.

'Romaine—she's not——?'

'Oh no, she's fine now,' she assured him. 'She was having an attack and suddenly went into cardiac arrest. It was lucky that I was there. She's had a lot of shocks over the last twenty-four hours, and it must have all been too much for her. I asked Edna to ring you because Adam was out, but he's with her now.'

Otto looked relieved. 'I'm so thankful that she had a trained nurse as companion,' he said. 'Between ourselves, my dear, I wish there were some way I could persuade her to give up the idea of this comeback she's so set on. But I've no doubt you know what she's like when her mind is made up.'

Leane knew only too well, and when she returned to the bedroom a little later with the hot water bottles Romaine was proving the point. As she opened the door she heard her saying: 'No, I insist that you hear me out. I cannot rest until I've said what I *must* say!'

Leane tucked the bottles at her feet, glad to see that she was looking much more herself. Romaine's eyes met hers as she went on:

'I've had another attack, haven't I?' She looked at the three closed faces round the bed and when no one spoke she said, 'Well, why don't you admit it? Your silence is as good as saying so. I knew what was coming when the pain hit me. Leane——' she held out her hand. 'I believe I might have died if it hadn't been for you. I'm not afraid of dying, but I'd been thinking about something you said earlier, when we were having dinner. What frightened me was that I might die without putting things right.' She turned to

Otto. 'Many years ago I believe I did you a great wrong.'

He shook his head. 'That cannot be so, my dear.'

'Oh, but it is.' She reached for his hand. 'In those far-off days we loved each other very much, didn't we?' she whispered.

He pressed her fingers and raised them to his lips. 'Very much, my dearest.'

'But when you left England to return to Austria there was something you didn't know—something I deliberately kept from you because I thought it might wreck your life and your career. A few months later, Otto, I gave birth to our son.'

Leane heard a small gasp escape Adam's lips and she looked up to see the look of incredulity on his face. Romaine smiled at him gently.

'You have always wanted to know, Adam. I should have told you both years ago.'

She stopped talking abruptly, obviously exhausted, and Leane poured her a glass of water from the carafe by the bed. There was a moment's shocked silence as the two men stared at each other across the bed and Leane took the opportunity to creep from the room. This moment, she told herself, belonged to the three of them. Adam would know where to find her if he felt like talking.

It was almost an hour later that she heard the light tap on her door and opened it to find Adam waiting outside.

'You weren't asleep—I didn't wake you?'

She shook her head. 'No, I half expected you.'

She looked at him as she closed the door. 'What a day! It seems more like a week since I got up this morning.'

He nodded. 'It's certainly a day I shan't forget in a hurry.' He reached out and drew her close. 'But I couldn't go to sleep without seeing you. I've been talking with my—with Otto.' He laughed. 'I don't think I'll ever get used to calling him "Father". I realised earlier this evening that there was a little more to him than met the eye. He's been telling me of a clinic he runs in Zurich for less wealthy people, especially children injured in accidents. It seems it's subsidised by the clinic here. He's offered me the job of senior surgeon there.'

Leane kissed him. 'Oh, Adam, how wonderful!'

'Of course it won't be for some time,' he went on. 'The present surgeon is due for retirement soon, though. There will be my job in London to wind up, and of course I would be working here with Otto for a while.' He looked down at her. 'There will be a job for you too if you want it, both here and in Zurich—as well as the job of being Mrs Adam Blake, I mean.'

She shook her head. 'It's almost too much to take in. But what about Romaine? She'll need someone.'

He smiled. 'It rather looks as though she'll be getting a husband. I have a feeling Otto won't let her get away this time. He's staying the night, by the way, and tomorrow he's getting in touch with a cardiologist friend in Geneva. He's absolutely determined to get her to give up the idea of making a comeback too.' He laughed. 'Romaine has met her match this time. From now on Otto will be making the decisions.'

'I think he's a wonderful man,' Leane said. 'I've thought so from the moment I met him. It's very strange to think he'll soon be my father-in-law. It's so long since I had a whole family of my own.' She sighed. 'To think that when I came here I only——'

But her words were lost as his lips covered hers. They stood together in the centre of the room, swaying slightly with tiredness, neither of them able to break away. Adam sighed and buried his face in her hair.

'It's almost morning, yet I can't bear to leave you. There's so much to say—so many plans to make. When I think of all the stupid mis-understandings—all the wasted time.'

Her arms tightened round him and she brushed her lips against his cheek. She was thinking about Romaine and Otto, of all the sacrifice and heartache, of the years that could never be recovered. 'We have plenty of time, darling,' she whispered. 'All the time in the world.'

He kissed her. 'Yet if we live to be a hundred there will never be a night like this,' he said softly.

Leane reached out her hand and switched off the light. Across the valley the first streaks of dawn cast their pearly light over the mountain tops as she melted in Adam's arms. He was right, there never would be a night quite like this.

The little English church by the lake was bright and fragrant with flowers on the day three weeks later when Leane became Mrs Adam Blake. She wore a dress of white chiffon which Romaine had delightedly helped her to choose and the bouquet she carried was made of Otto's celebrated Iceberg roses. Stan had proudly given her away and Otto had been Adam's best man. He had agreed on condition that Adam returned the compliment the following month, at his own wedding to Romaine. Bridget had flown over for the wedding as a special surprise laid on by Romaine. She had arrived the night before and after the small reception at the chalet she retired with Leane to help her change into her going-away clothes. As the bedroom door closed behind them she hugged Leane.

'Oh, it's been such a *lovely* wedding! Who would have guessed that all this would happen when you applied for the job?' She sighed. 'Fate took a hand there right enough. When I saw the papers that morning with the story about Romaine's operation I expected to see you back on the next plane. I thought it might have blown the whole thing!'

'It almost did,' Leane told her. 'But in fact it seemed as though it simply started the ball rolling. Once that secret was out the others followed. I don't think Romaine would ever have stood up to that comeback. The attack she had may well have saved her life in more ways than one.'

'And now she's getting married too—to her first love.' Bridget sighed. 'Oh isn't it *romantic*?' She zipped up the cream linen dress that Leane had stepped into. 'Where did you say you were going for your honeymoon?'

Leane laughed. 'I didn't—but it's a little ski-lodge that Otto owns. It's away up high in the mountains, and we shall have it all to ourselves for two whole weeks.' She caught sight of Bridget's wistful face in the mirror and turned to hug her. 'When we've set up our home in Zurich you must come and stay for long holidays,' she promised.

'I shall look forward to that.' The other girl's eyes filled with tears. 'It's lovely to see you looking so happy. I'm so glad for you, and I think Adam is just *gorgeous*.'

The door opened and Adam's head came round it. 'Time's getting on, Lee. Are you ready?'

Bridget kissed Leane's cheek. 'I'll go down and tell them you're coming. See you in a minute.'

When she had gone Adam held out his arms. 'Well, Mrs Blake, how does it feel to be alone with your husband?'

She went to him and put her arms round his waist. 'It feels slightly unbelievable, but I daresay I'll get used to the idea.' She lifted her face for his kiss and for a long moment they stood wrapped in a happy glow.

'They'll be waiting—we'd better go,' Leane warned at last.

Adam sighed. 'You're right. Goodness only knows what they'll be thinking.' He laughed and tucked her hand through his arm, but as they reached the door she stopped, remembering something.

'My bouquet—I have to throw it. Romaine would never forgive me if I didn't give her the chance to catch her favourite flowers. They're her symbol of happiness.'

She picked up the bouquet of delicate wax-like blooms from the dressing table and whirled happily out of the room, leaving it still alive with her happiness—still fragrant with the scent of the Iceberg rose.

Doctor Nurse Romances

Don't miss
January's
other story of love and romance amid the pressure
and emotion of medical life.

THE GEMEL RING
by Betty Neels

Charity disliked and despised Everard van Tijlen, the eminent Dutch surgeon whose fees were so outrageously expensive. Then she found herself working with him — and her ideas began to change!

Order your copy today from your local paperback retailer.

Doctor Nurse Romances

and February's
stories of romantic relationships behind the scenes
of modern medical life are:

HEARTACHE HOSPITAL
by Lynne Collins

Staff Nurse Jessica Brook has known and loved Clive Mortimer ever since she started nursing at Heartlake Hospital. But the action she takes, after seeing him fooling around with a first-year nurse again, means that Heartlake turns quickly into Heartache Hospital...

NURSE SMITH, COOK
by Joyce Dingwell

Nurse Fiona Smith has looked after her young nephew ever since his mother's death — and is determined to continue doing so after his father insists he joins him in Australia. But the boy's father stipulates 'no accompanying women' so on arrival she pretends to be his new cook instead...

Order your copies today from your local paperback retailer